THE PRINCESS BRIDE OF RIODAN

ECHO RIDGE ROMANCE #3

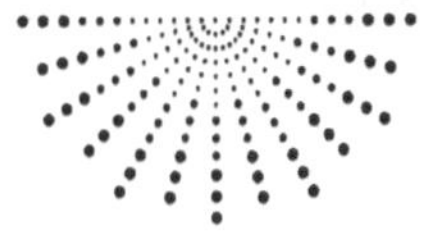

RACHELLE J. CHRISTENSEN

Praise for

Claire's Christmas Dance

ISBN: 978-1-949319-11-8

The Princess Bride of Riodan: An Echo Ridge Romance

Original Cover Design: Steven Novak

Cover Design © Peachwood Press

Published by Peachwood Press, March 2018

❀ Created with Vellum

Get your free book!

Thrills for the Heart

FOR A LIMITED TIME

Sign up for Rachelle's
VIP Mailing List
to get your *FREE* book.

★ ★ ★ ★ ★

Get started here:
www.rachellechristensen.com

To the ladies of Echo Ridge: Heather, Cami, Lucy, Connie, and Janette. Thank you for making this town a place that I wish I could visit! It's been such a joy to work with each of you and learn from your creative talents.

Dear Reader,

I'm delighted you've come back to visit the town of Echo Ridge, New York! If this is your first visit, I'm glad to have you! Each book in the Echo Ridge Romance series can be read as a stand-alone.

In this third book of the series, you'll discover the story of Elise Gibson and a very interesting prince.

The title of my story hints at a favorite movie that I still enjoy watching today. However, the storyline has nothing to do with the movie. I hope fans of the movie will enjoy all of the quotable lines and fun phrases that might be familiar.

I hope you'll be reminded of favorite times watching movies and reading books with your friends and family as you get to know Elise and her town.

Thank you for investing your time to read my book. I am so grateful for your support! You are the reason I write. If you enjoy this book, please consider leaving a review at your favorite online store. Each and every one helps me as an author.

Thank you and happy reading!

Rachelle

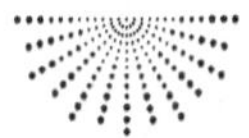

Wallpaper. Not just any wallpaper, but the kind that incited nightmares, covered every wall of the basement in the old Emerald Inn, Echo Ridge's premiere Bed & Breakfast. Elise Gibson ran the steamer along another section of the navy blue design with pink and maroon paisley and little golden flourishes that had real gold-leafing overlaid on the expensive textured wallpaper. Thirty years ago, this room had been part of the owner's separate living quarters and it was the height of interior design. Now it was up to Elise to remodel the large area into a stylish home theater where guests of the B&B could come and enjoy their favorite movies. The room would cater to the wealthy guests of Echo Ridge, New York, during the ski season and during the off-season it would be available for party rentals for the locals.

The steamer hissed and Elise pulled down one long section of the hideous wallpaper. The owners had used quality paper—thick as denim and caked in glue. She checked her watch. It was almost eight o'clock and since it was the last Tuesday of March, she needed to be to Kenworth's department store by nine to help decorate the window for the annual Tulip festival. She crumpled the paper into a ball and threw it aside. Stepping back, she smiled at the wall. It was yellowed and would need a good scrubbing, but the original texture would look fabulous with a new coat of paint. There were still three more walls to uncover in the eight-hundred square foot room, but Elise was up for the challenge. First, she needed to pack up the rest of the DVDs on the bookshelf.

The room had been semi-functioning as a movie room and lounge area for guests and the family that ran the place. There was an old oak bookcase with several dents that held about a hundred titles. Elise grabbed an empty box and knelt next to the bottom shelf. She stacked two dozen Disney movies inside and moved to the next shelf. When she pulled off the next DVD a sigh escaped before she could stop it. *The Princess Bride* was definitely a love story worth repeating. She'd probably watched that movie twenty times with her mother that last summer before she died. Elise had just turned fourteen and her mom was thirty-six—too young to die of a heart attack. After her mom died, Elise's dad who resembled Prince Humperdink in more ways than appearance, sent Elise and her younger brother to Echo Ridge to live with their grandma. It was the best thing that could've happened to her. She carefully set the movie into the box, wishing that a man like Westley existed off the silver screen.

Bonnie Montgomery, one half of the dynamic duo who owned and managed the B&B, definitely had good cinematic taste. One entire shelf was filled with old chick flicks that Elise considered required viewing as a rite of passage for life. She packed up *You've Got Mail, My Best Friend's Wedding, Runaway Bride, While You Were Sleeping,* and even *My Fair Lady.* Elise smiled and hurried to empty the rest of the bookshelf. She put the box of movies into a closet and gathered up the wads of wallpaper from the floor. Trudging up the servant's staircase at the back of the B&B brought her to a landing near the south entrance. Elise opened the door and stepped out, carefully pulling it shut behind her without dropping the remains of the wallpaper. She felt for the next step with her foot, but just as she made contact with the stair she ran into something solid.

As she started to tip sideways, someone grabbed her around the waist, lifted her from the steps and set her down. "Got you there," the man said, his voice sounded muffled.

That was probably because Elise was clutching the wallpaper so tight, the edges of the wad were caught in her hair. "My goodness, I'm sorry," she said as she lowered the paper and looked up to meet the gaze of the man she'd tumbled into. He was definitely not what Elise was expecting to see that morning. His dark skin and black curly hair glistened with a sheen of perspiration. He was shirtless with bright orange running shorts. And he had muscles. Lots of big muscles. Elise forced herself to focus on his eyes, thinking that would be better than staring at his finely toned pectorals and biceps, but it didn't help. His eyes were so brown, they were almost black and they were rimmed with eyelashes any woman would kill for.

Neither of them were saying anything, which for him might be normal, but Elise wasn't even speechless in her sleep. His deep brown eyes bore into hers and she almost took a step back before realizing that the stairs she'd almost fallen down were still behind her.

"I'm sorry if I scared you," he finally said, backing up a step. "I didn't want you to fall."

His voice was quiet, cultured, and yes—definitely exotic. Elise could just catch the hint of an accent on his words. She wanted to ask if he was foreign, but he seemed a bit more reserved and she didn't want to pry or appear rude.

She swallowed. "Thank you. I'm sorry I wasn't

looking where I was going. Actually I couldn't see even if I was looking over this pile of horrid wallpaper. I've been taking it down to remodel the theater room in the basement. I still don't understand how navy and pink paisley could have ever been in style. It's a huge job. You're tall so you'd have no problem reaching the top of the wall, but I have to use a stepladder and that is kind of precarious with a steamer." She scrunched the ball of wallpaper she still held and clamped her mouth shut. She hadn't really just said all that to a complete stranger, had she? It looked like he was trying hard not to smile. Yep, that was her—open mouth and dump every conscious thought into a form of speech.

"So, you work here?" he asked.

"Not all the time. I'm an interior decorator and they hired me for this project. I'm heading over to Kenworth's in a minute to set up the window display and then I'll work a few hours at Paisley's Petals—my other job is at the flower shop. How about you? What brings you here?"

"Oh, I was just out for a run." He breathed in deep and Elise noted his fine lung capacity—at least it probably was pretty good considering the size of his chest.

"This is a beautiful time of year to be outside. I just love it when I catch the smell of hyacinths. They're my favorite, but they never last long enough, you know?"

He smiled and his teeth were a bright white contrast to his dark skin. "I don't really know that flower."

"Hang on, I'll show you." She stepped past him and dumped the crumpled wallpaper in the garbage. Then she turned and motioned to him. "Right over here." The spring morning was brisk and she wondered if he was cold, or maybe not judging by the sheen of perspiration on his dark skin.

She walked across the grass to an oval-shaped flowerbed that surrounded a beautiful Linden tree. "See these light purple and dark pink flowers?" Elise crouched and pointed at the flowers. "These are hyacinths."

"Ah, I have seen those a few times before." The man nodded.

"But have you smelled them? Come here, you have to crouch down to get close enough to catch the aroma. There's nothing like it." Elise motioned with her hand and she noticed the side of his dimpled cheek twitch as if he was trying not to smile again. He crouched down and sniffed and then looked over at her, surprise widening his dark eyes.

"That scent...it's almost like my aunt's favorite perfume." He leaned in again and inhaled deeply.

"She must have good taste then," Elise replied. She straightened and he stood next to her. "My name's Elise Gibson. Sorry to trip over you and then take you on a botany lesson, but I'm so glad you like hyacinths too, or at least your aunt must."

He let out a laugh and the musical quality in his voice shot a thrill through Elise's middle. "I like them too. She is my favorite aunt and I don't get to see her very often. But the next time I do, I'll try to bring her some of these hyacinths."

Elise tucked her hair behind her ear. The dark curls fell past her shoulder and stuck to the back of her neck. The morning chill had left and the man with no shirt and too many muscles might have had something to do with that. "Hopefully that will be soon because these flowers will only be here for about two weeks."

"I'd better hurry then. The flower shop you mentioned, do they carry these hyacinths?"

"Special order for the next two weeks," Elise replied. "Oh, and I usually have some business cards with a ten percent discount, but if you stop by today while I'm working I can get you one of those."

"Oh, I wouldn't want to trouble you," he replied. "Thank you for your kindness this morning. I'd better be on my way." He lifted his chin with a smile and turned to go.

Elise started to wave. "Wait. Who are you?"

He opened his mouth as if to answer and then hesitated. His smile morphed into a thin line. He shrugged. "No one of consequence."

Elise stepped forward, putting her hand on his arm. She'd probably scared him off with her constant chatter and too much information about flowers, but there was something about him that was more than finely sculpted abs and a dazzling smile. She looked into his eyes. "I must know."

He swallowed and took a deep breath. He studied her face and a small line formed between his brow before he glanced down at her hand and stepped away from her touch. The corner of his mouth turned up in a half-smile and he winked. "Get used to disappointment." Before she could say another word, he sprinted across the lawn.

"Okay, that was rude," Elise said, but she smiled anyway as she watched the rhythm of his perfect shoulders in sync with his steps as he ran down the road. So he wanted to save wallpapered damsels in distress and be mysterious at the same time? That was fine with Elise, because she loved a good mystery.

CHAPTER TWO

Prince Weston Montoya of Riodan tried to concentrate on counting his steps per minute as he pounded the pavement south of Echo Ridge Main Street. He'd almost told that woman who he was. He gritted his teeth.

Once Elise started talking, he'd spent most of the time trying not to smile at the way her eyes sparkled and her cheeks lifted as she rattled off more words than he usually spoke in a day. She had him sniffing flowers and talking of Aunt Jacinta. And he'd handed over the information like a rookie prince who didn't know better than to protect the family's private information. Then she'd asked him who he was. He'd let his guard down and almost ruined everything and instead of acting debonair and giving a fake name, like he usually did, he'd turned tail and run. *Nothing suspicious about that.* He clenched his fist and ducked his head, running harder. He probably wouldn't see her again, but a part of him wanted to turn back around and continue their conversation. Instead, he ran farther away. Elise was an American, so she was off-limits.

Weston was the youngest prince from a large royal family that inhabited a small island east of the Bermuda Triangle. Riodan was rich in oil, diamonds, and gold yet had kept a low profile for hundreds of years. At least they had until Weston's brother, Titan, decided to open up an account for every type of social media ever invented and document the latest nanosecond of his life in pictures. For the past three months, the royal compound had been crawling with paparazzi drooling over the hidden gem of the Atlantic Ocean—the Montoya family.

His cell phone buzzed, interrupting his thoughts. He pulled his phone from the pocket of his running shorts and glanced at the screen. He grimaced at the photo of his mother smiling as if she couldn't hurt a fly and she wouldn't, but he was in for a tongue lashing. Might as well get it over with it.

"Good morning," Weston said, slowing his pace.

"It might be a good morning if a mother knew where her son was hiding. Queen Raeni of Riodan has always prided herself on the honor of her family."

Uh-oh, she was already talking in third person. That

was never a good sign. "Mother, I know you're worried, but please don't. I'm fine. Once all of this mess with Titan blows over, I'll return, but things have to change from now on. I can't live like that anymore."

There were two beats of silence. "You're forsaking the crown? The royal family? All that your father has worked for?"

Weston groaned. "What crown? Titan is the crown prince and then Zac, and Marius, not to mention Ayida and Marisha. The only thing I'll be ruling is the royal dog house and even Sheba won't bow to me."

Queen Raeni made a noise that sounded like she was trying not to laugh. For all of her regal and royal under-pinnings, his mother had a good sense of humor. "You are a Montoya which means that you are part of the royal family. I suggest you revisit your lineage and the qualifications and requirements that go along with it. Azzaca was never a contender for the crown and with the choices that Titan is making, I doubt he will be much longer. Marius, however, could make a good king."

"Wait, that stuff is ancient history," Wes said. "No one really goes by those rules and you and Dad can make amendments to the clause about the true heir of the kingdom." Even though he would never be ruler of Riodan, Wes still felt responsible for his country.

His mother tsked. "You are only twenty-eight, so it

might not make sense to follow *ancient* protocol but I would again remind you to study the history that you must have skipped in your sixteenth year. Haggarik was the worst tutor we ever employed and I'm sorry to recognize just what it might have cost you."

Weston stopped running and leaned against a lamp post. "Mother, I'm not sure I understand what you're saying."

"You don't," she replied, "and this is a delicate conversation best saved for a time when you have studied and prepared."

Weston clenched his teeth, pulling in a breath through his nose. His mother always seemed to be playing some kind of game. "Fine, I'll call Father and ask him to explain it to me."

"I wouldn't do that if I were you, at least not until you finish your studies. He has quite enough to deal with right now. Titan had a misunderstanding with a police officer last night and your father is trying to work it out."

Weston huffed. "I'm sorry to hear that. I won't bother either of you and I'm keeping a low profile, so don't worry." It had been weird walking the streets without his armed guards to accompany him. Part of him felt a relief he'd never experienced while a part that he'd never admit felt exposed and vulnerable.

"I'm your mother, it's my job to worry," she replied. "I

love you, Weston. I want you to be happy and I also want you to realize what you have."

"Thanks, Mother. I'll talk to you soon, okay?"

"Kiss, kiss," his mother whispered before ending the call.

Weston turned and started running back along the quiet streets where shop owners were getting ready to start the day. He mulled over the conversation with his mother. She loved to toy with people, hint, cajole, and raise curiosities and suspicions, but she never teased about the royal family requirements. What did she mean that Titan, the crown prince, might not be king of Riodan and the next son in line, Azacca, was never a contender for the crown? This was part of the reason he'd snuck out of the country. He needed a chance to get his bearings and figure out who he was without ancient royal protocol dictating his every move. He wasn't sure how many weeks it would take for him to achieve the balance he sought. Hopefully, Echo Ridge would be a safe haven for the next month. He had a project to complete that required no interruptions from the paparazzi. Weston shook his head. It was too much to think about on an empty stomach.

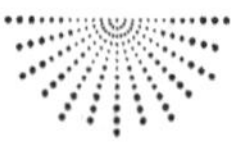

That Tuesday after work when Elise pulled open the mailbox a stack of letters waited for her. She peered inside the dented yellow mailbox with a frown. She didn't like seeing letters—at least the kind that came in long business envelopes with cellophane windows. Bills. She would much rather see a furniture ad or coupon flier. She couldn't think of the last time she'd received an actual hand-written letter or card. Elise pursed her lips and flipped through the stack. They were mostly addressed to Suzette Gibson, otherwise known as her Grandma Suzy.

Elise's stomach clenched when she saw the red "Past Due" notice stamped on the outside of the letter with the county assessor's return address. Property taxes had been the source of many sleepless nights for Grandma Suzy and several upset stomachs for Elise. With slumped shoulders, Elise turned toward her home, the grand three-story house that was built over one-hundred years ago by her great-great-great grandfather Amos Gibson. Back then, there wasn't such a thing as property taxes that drained the fixed income of the elderly and put a strain on the meager income of the young and inexperienced.

"Elise, I didn't know you were home. You've had a phone call," Grandma called from the front porch.

Elise clasped the letters in her hand and forced the corners of her mouth upwards. "Hi Gran, how are you feeling today?"

Grandma rubbed at her elbow. "I think a storm will be here before next week."

Elise shook her head. "It's springtime, of course it will storm in upstate New York, but probably before tomorrow." Elise glanced upward at the blue sky dotted with puffy white clouds. Living in Echo Ridge was a dream Elise had held onto when everyone had told her she'd be better off to venture to the big city and make her mark as an interior designer. Spring rainstorms pouring off the newly budding maple trees in a small town were one of the many things she loved.

Grandma shook her finger at Elise brand tsked. "You little whippersnappers think you know everything with your new-fangled devices." She rubbed her elbow again and muttered. "We'll see who has the last umbrella by next week."

Elise laughed and pecked Grandma on the cheek. They had an ongoing friendly competition to see who was more accurate in predicting the weather—the app on her cell phone or Gran's elbow. "So who called?"

"Funny thing. At first I thought they had it wrong but it was The Emerald Inn downtown."

"Was it Bonnie?"

"Yes, that was her name. She said something about a job you were doing there. Honey, I thought you already had two jobs."

Elise sucked in a breath. Gran was concerned about how much she worked, and she blamed herself for not being able to provide for her grandchildren better. It was easy for her brother Mark to assure Gran that he was doing fine with his full-ride scholarship to Texas A&M University and didn't need any extra money. Mark was also removed from the stresses of getting bills in the mail with late notices. But Elise lived here, so she would have to spin the job as an opportunity, not a means to come up with enough to pay the property taxes. "Bonnie and Roy Montgomery hired me to redecorate the theater room there." She rose on her tiptoes and smiled. "It's a great opportunity to add experience to my portfolio and I can't wait to show you my ideas."

Grandma chuckled. "Go on then. You can tell me all about it over dinner."

Elise linked arms with Gran and walked inside the house. The aroma of her homemade chicken noodle soup made Elise's stomach stand to attention. Life didn't seem so difficult when she had a full belly of Gran's thick homemade noodles and creamy soup. "Thanks for making dinner again."

Gran turned to her and smiled. "Thanks for being here."

The next morning Elise was back at the B&B to continue her war on ugly wallpaper. She plugged in the steamer and waited a few minutes for the water to heat. It really was a two-person job, but Elise needed the money for the property taxes. She had always been resourceful and with a step ladder and a little balance she was able to steam the top section of the wallpaper, loosen it and move to the lower portion of the wall.

She steamed the edge of the thick paper and it began to peel. With satisfaction, she pulled the paper forward as she continued to steam away the glue on the bottom half of the wall. The section of paper was nearly three feet wide and Elise let it billow over the top of her and the ladder as she climbed down another step and pulled the paper off.

"Looks like you could use a hand," someone said from the back stairwell. Elise turned and nearly fell off the stepladder. It was the same man from yesterday, but he was fully dressed today. She pushed the wallpaper off her head.

"You!" She grabbed onto the ladder and bent over. "Don't sneak up on me like that!"

"Sorry about that." He walked up to the ladder and put his large hand on the frame to steady it. His cheek twitched as he tried not to smile. He looked good in stone-washed jeans and a dark blue t-shirt. "Can I help you somehow?"

She returned her attention to the navy blue wallpaper in front of her. "Well, as much fun as this looks. I'm sure you have better things to do on a Wednesday morning."

"Actually, I have no idea what you are doing. I've never seen a machine like that before."

She started laughing. She climbed down from the ladder, still chuckling. Holding up the steamer, she said, "This is a steamer. The machine heats water to boiling and the steam travels through this tube and when I put the paddle on the wallpaper, the steam comes out, breaks down the glue and then I can pull the paper off like this." She tugged on the sheet of paper and the section she'd just been steaming came loose.

He looked from her to the steamer and then to the paper. "So strange. They don't use wallpaper in my home."

"And where is that?" Elise asked.

He opened his mouth, closed it, and turned back to the wallpaper. "Nowhere of consequence, but I'd like to try this. Can I?"

"I don't want you to spend your limited vacation time helping in the basement. You should be out in the beautiful springtime weather of Echo Ridge, taking in the sights, and eating one of Fay's cinnamon rolls."

"It is a nice town. I'll have to check out Fay's, but first, are you going to let me help you?"

She raised her eyebrows and handed him the paddle. Bonnie and Roy had told her to be polite to the guests as some of them were eccentric. That was the only thing keeping her from peppering him with more questions. "You slide the paddle across the surface. Don't keep it in one place too long or it will cause the paint to bubble beneath the wallpaper."

He smiled and held the paddle. "You Americans do the strangest things to your homes." So he was foreign. She could still hear a trace of an accent rounding out the end of his words, but she couldn't place it.

She leaned across him and put a hand on top of his,

pushing the paddle across the paper a bit faster. "Like this. That's good. Now lift the paddle off, keeping it away from your face and pull that section of the wallpaper toward you."

He tugged on the paper and grinned as the whole section came off the wall.

"There, you've successfully steamed wallpaper." Elise took the paddle from him, ready to continue with her work. "When you return from your vacation, you can tell all your friends."

His smile dissolved into a thin line. Elise wondered if she'd said something wrong or maybe the guy didn't have friends. He shook his head and forced the smile back onto his face. "Thank you. Could I help you on that top section? That ladder doesn't seem like the safest option." The way he studied the paddle she held with curiosity and a mixture of excitement made it impossible for Elise to say no. She handed it over.

"Suit yourself. I'll be steaming the rest of these walls today. Maybe I should put out a sign and see if I get any more interested tourists who want to help."

He laughed. "A good idea." He reached up and put the paddle near the ceiling. "Fast enough?" he asked as he moved it across the wall.

She nodded. When he started pulling the paper down, Elise couldn't help it. She'd never liked biting her tongue, it was painful. It hurt her brain not to say what she wanted to. "Why so cryptic?"

He tilted his head, a confused look on his face.

Elise rolled her eyes. "Your name. I still don't know your name."

"Oh, that," he coughed. "It's Wes. Sorry I didn't introduce myself."

She was about to say something snarky about that not being a real introduction, when he pointed at the corner of the paper beginning to peel. "Do you mind if I pull this section down as you steam? I think it would come off a lot easier."

"Not at all. Thank you."

He was at least six foot, if not a couple inches more and he easily reached the top of the wall and pulled the paper toward him. When he reached a point where the paper resisted, Elise held up her hand. "Wait, let me steam that section again. Some of this glue wasn't evenly spread across the wall when they put on this paper. My grandma Suzy said she's pretty sure this paper was here when she was raising kids—over thirty years ago." Elise stepped back and let Wes pull the paper down. "It kind of makes me sad, like I'm removing part of history. Of course, it helps that it's so ugly. But still, don't you wonder about the people who originally lived in this mansion? They must have had so many hopes and dreams and grand ideas. I've lived in Echo Ridge most of my life, but I don't know much about the original owners of this place."

Wes stared at her with a half-smile as he wadded up the paper.

"Sorry, I should've warned you that I talk a lot." And she especially talked a lot when incredibly handsome men helped her remove wallpaper. Wes had nice biceps —his dark skin was sculpted and toned all the way down to the backs of his hands. It made her middle feel gooey and warm like one of Grandma Suzy's chocolate chip cookies. He tossed the pile of paper into the corner and turned back to her. "I don't mind. I have a couple sisters who like to talk non-stop too."

"Really? I never had a sister. I do have a younger brother, but Mark lives in Texas and won't graduate from college for another couple years. I don't get to see him much. You're lucky to have so much family around. Are they older or younger than you?"

He looked at the ground and breathed in and out slowly. Then he raised his head and met her gaze, his eyes seemed darker—almost black. "I don't really want to talk about myself right now, if that's okay."

"Well, you're the one who brought it up." Elise looked at him for a moment, but he averted his eyes. She shrugged. "As you wish."

He cocked an eyebrow at her, but didn't say anything. Elise thought for sure he would leave, but he just reached up and began tugging at the next section of wallpaper. They finished removing the paper off the next wall. At first Elise tried not to say much to punish him for being a closed book, but her tongue got the best of her before long. They ended up talking about all sorts of things that didn't reveal much about his personal life, but did reveal a lot about his personality. Wes liked creating things, being on the move, and accomplishing goals. He talked about wanting to own a business someday.

"What kind of business?" Elise asked.

"I don't know for sure. I have so many interests, it's hard to narrow it down to one thing." His eyes sparkled as he talked and Elise could tell that he was being genuine, not holding back in this moment of the conversation.

"I know what you mean. My grandma keeps telling me that I need to focus on one thing and do it well, but that's so boring. I mean, I get to work with all sorts of decorations, flowers, and make things look beautiful inside and out. I like being spontaneous. I think I'd die if I had to do the same thing day after day."

She turned back to look at Wes. He smiled, the dimple in his right cheek twitching.

"What?"

"You *do* talk a lot."

Elise didn't even blush. She'd accepted that conversational quirk about herself long ago. "Thank you."

Wes chuckled. "You're welcome."

"You know, one time I even tried my hand at dog-walking," Elise continued as if she didn't notice how Wes watched her mouth as she spoke. "I returned the dogs to the wrong houses so it was short-lived."

When the steamer ran out of water, Wes was laughing so hard she didn't hear the clicking noise on the machine. He set the paddle down and stepped closer to Elise. "Thanks for this." He motioned to the wall and patted her arm. "I needed some stress relief today."

He had a great smile—it elicited the feel-good vibes she got when she ate chocolate-covered cinnamon bears from the Candy Counter. And the little zip of energy she felt when he touched her arm felt good too. "Thank you for making a boring job so much easier."

"My pleasure." Wes looked directly in her eyes like he was searching for something.

She smiled and leaned toward him, whispering. "My eyes are pretty green, huh?"

Wes chuckled and leaned in closer. "They are beautiful, like you're filled with light."

The air between them arced with an invisible force that seemed to pull them closer. His eyes searching hers for an answer to a question that he wouldn't voice. His gaze dropped to her mouth and he swallowed, but instead of leaning down, he slowly straightened to his full height.

"Thank you," Elise murmured. What had just happened? She didn't dare ask, but she wanted to say, 'Were you about to kiss me? Because I'd love to kiss you but I need to know your last name first.' Maybe if they spent a little more time together. An idea popped into her mind and she was speaking before she even finished the thought. "Hey, would you like to grab lunch at Fay's with me and a few friends today?"

Wes froze and the smile slipped from his face. "I'm sorry. I'd like to, but I can't." He glanced at his watch. "I've spent more time than I should have here. Please excuse me, but I need to go."

"Oh, no problem," Elise replied, nodding her head several times. She probably looked like a bobble-head doll. "Have a great day and thanks again for your help."

Wes hesitated, opening his mouth as if he were about to say something, and then clamped it shut. He gave a hurried goodbye, left the room, and then she heard him dashing up the stairs. She stared at the piles of wallpaper, feeling like he'd just stolen all of her chocolate-covered cinnamon bears.

CHAPTER FOUR

Thursday came and went in Elise's crammed schedule without a visit to the B&B. On Friday afternoon when she'd finally finished up her duties at the flower shop, she almost ran to her car. What if Wes had already checked out? She had a craving for him that she shouldn't indulge in, but every other hour yesterday, she was thinking of him and reliving their conversations. He was a bit mysterious, but Elise figured it was only a matter of time until he let his guard down and invited her to get to know him. Right now they were on a first name basis—well, maybe not even that, since Wes was most likely a nickname for Wesley or something.

It was two thirty by the time she arrived and Elise kept telling herself that chances were slim she would see him. Most guests had checked out and the B&B was waiting eagerly for the new weekend guests to check in. Bonnie's son Carter was hard at work in the backyard finishing up a gazebo for a wedding. When Elise walked in the lobby she heard the phone ringing and overheard the clerk answering, "Hello, my name is Ingrid Montgomery. Your reservation is ready, prepare to be delighted."

Elise smiled. Ingrid was Roy's niece and fit right in with the rest of the family working at the B&B. Elise walked down the hallway, nearly running into Bonnie bustling down the stairs with an armful of towels.

"Good afternoon," Bonnie said brightly. Before Elise could even answer, Bonnie raised her eyebrows. "Oh! Elise, I needed to tell you something."

"Yes?"

"It's important," she said in a hushed tone. "I meant to tell you that we have a very important guest staying with us. I'm certain I can trust you to be discreet with this information. I normally wouldn't say a word, but it's likely you'll run into him with as much time as you'll be spending here."

Elise nodded, trying not to appear too eager, but her curiosity was piqued.

Bonnie swallowed. "Royalty. He's registered under a fake name but I'd know him anywhere. It's one of the Montoya brothers. Not the crown prince, mind you, but there's a security detail that came snooping through here right after he arrived and they check in every day. Dead giveaway if you ask me."

"Wait a minute. There's a prince staying here in Echo Ridge?" Elise had noticed several guests coming and going, but none of them looked like royalty. That was probably the point though, to blend in. She could have spoken with the prince and not even realized it.

"And he looks a lot like his brother, Titan—too handsome for his own good. Well, I'd better be going," Bonnie said. "Remember what I said and oh—speak of the devil. There he is!"

Elise looked up and gasped when she saw Wes crossing the street in front of the B&B. "No, that can't be him."

"But it is," Bonnie whispered. "See those two men across the street? They're his guards. He doesn't even act like he knows them. Nice fellow though."

The bell above the door chimed as Wes entered and Elise stood there gaping. She locked eyes with Wes. She looked behind him so pointedly that he turned and glanced back at the street. He was a prince. And not just any prince—a Montoya from the isle of Riodan. Gran followed Prince Titan on Facebook—as did most of the world. Now all of his cryptic answers and mysterious withholding of information made sense. She didn't like it when people pretended to be something they weren't.

Wes turned back around and took a step forward. "How's the wallpaper today?" he asked cheerfully.

Elise felt her face flush. She folded her arms and gave him a cold stare. "Just peachy. I'll be finished later today. I'm heading to another job first." She turned and walked through the reception area and out the back door, her plans changing with the arc of her emotions. She couldn't talk to him right now, not if he really was a prince. She jogged out to her car and climbed inside. There were a couple of things she wanted to adjust on the Kenworth's window display for the tulip festival. She'd come back to the B&B later.

Her chest heaved and she swallowed hot tears in the back of her throat. Why was she so upset? Well, besides the fact that she'd never be able to show her face again once the Montgomerys found out she'd had a prince working in the basement. Maybe it wasn't true. Bonnie was known to let her imagination run away with her. Elise pulled out her cell phone and searched for a picture of the royal family of Riodan. Headlines of the crown prince scorning the "island scum" were first and Elise shook her head with empathy for those people. Maybe Wes thought even less of her—working three jobs and not even aware that she had a prince taking down wallpaper.

She slid her finger across the screen filled with pictures, past his older brothers Titan, Azacca, and

Marius. And there he was waving at the photographer, a casual smile and that dimple. It really was him. Prince Weston—the royal that looked so much like his brother who had women flocking to the shores of Riodan after him.

Oh well, maybe she could get a picture of him before he left to remind her of the afternoon she'd spent teaching a prince how to remove wallpaper. Her heart twisted and she felt like she was in junior high all over again, crushing on the ninth grade boy who was way out of her league. Elise took a cleansing breath and decided that she would make this into a positive experience, but first she needed to get to work.

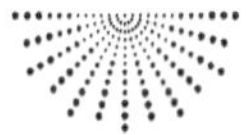

CHAPTER FIVE

Elise drove over to the park where the tulip festival would be held in less than one week. She wanted to get a feel for the area and make a few small adjustments to capture the atmosphere in her window display. Jessica, from the women's department, had already given her a few tips on how to integrate fresh flowers into the displays of spring clothing in the window. A line of brightly-colored wool scarves had added a pop of color when Jessica had shown Elise how to drape the scarves in several different fashions on the mannequins. Those same mannequins held baskets and painted tins full of silk tulips in every shade. Maybe the window was just fine and it was Elise's life that felt incomplete. With a sigh, she got out of her car and walked along the sidewalk.

When she stopped by the central flowerbed she

caught sight of a familiar crouching figure with a camera. Her best friend Amy McCallister was an excellent photographer and had a great eye for design as well. Amy's red hair cascaded down her back in ringlets, a contrast to Elise's dark brown hair. Amy was Irish-American and she loved her heritage. She had tons of family in New York with her Irish clan. Sometimes Elise felt like she'd been short-changed with her middle-class status and her lack of foreign ties.

"Amy, fancy seeing you here. What have you been up to?" Elise side-hugged her, avoiding the bulky camera.

"Well, I got a new wide angle lens that is to die for and when the credit card bill comes due next month, I probably will die."

"You bought something you don't have money to pay for?"

"Sort of. It was a deal I couldn't pass up and I've been saving but I didn't quite have the six-thousand dollar total."

Elise pretended to gag and choke. "Okay, let's talk about something else 'cause that's way too scary."

Amy laughed. "I've been taking lots of pictures for different online magazines and also working with my images to put them on some of the stock photo sites. Hopefully that will help with paying off my bills."

"See, your problem will be solved before you know it. You're so talented."

"Almost as talented as my designer friend."

Elise gazed past the park and could see the tip of the B&B in the distance. She frowned. She'd looked forward to seeing Wes today and now everything seemed gloomy.

"What's that grimace about?" Amy nudged her with her elbow.

Elise straightened and shook her head. "Oh, nothing. Just lots on my mind."

"Nope, not buyin' it. Little Miss Sunshine got rained on today but the skies look sunny to me, so what's the deal?"

Elise sighed. Amy had always been intuitive and they'd spent enough time together over the past couple years to recognize each other's moods. But Elise was supposed to be discreet.

"Well, I spent a bunch of time with this guy and he was kind of evasive about his personal information. We were mostly chatting, but I kind of thought we hit it off and then I found out, he wasn't who I thought he was.

"Wait a minute. Was he married?" Amy grabbed Elise's arm. "Were you seriously dating a married guy and didn't know it?"

"No, I wasn't dating anyone, just sort of hanging out," Elise protested. "And he wasn't married—isn't married."

"How do you know for sure?"

"Because I know."

Amy furrowed her brow. "So he gave you a fake name or what?"

"Sort of. He would only tell me his first name."

"And when you found out his last name it caused a problem?"

Elise groaned.

"Not married, no fake name, last name means something." Amy ticked off the words on her fingers. "So… let's see, he's the fairy-tale prince?"

"What? How did you know about the prince?" As the words tumbled out of her mouth, Elise realized that Amy had been joking.

Amy raised her eyebrows and held out her hand. "Spill it."

With a deep breath, Elise told Amy all about the handsome wallpaper assistant turned prince.

"Get out!" Amy said. "I can't believe that you were in the basement of the B&B with a prince." She pulled out her phone and within seconds had pulled up several different shots of Weston. "If he's half as gorgeous as he looks in these photos, I'd forgive him for being a prince and not telling."

Elise snatched Amy's phone away and scrolled through the pictures. Her stomach flipped when she recognized a grin that looked similar to one Wes had given her when they were working on wallpaper. Most of the shots of him consisted of the top of his head as he ducked to miss the camera. Or there were several profile shots as he turned away. "It seems like he doesn't like to be photographed."

"I could remedy that," Amy said. She lifted her camera. "I wonder how long he's staying in Echo Ridge."

"Amy, no, you could get me in a lot of trouble."

"With who? Bonnie? If she told you, then she told someone else and it only takes one leak to sink the boat." Amy watched her for a reaction. "Wait a minute? You really like him, don't you?"

Elise pulled her shoe through the grass. "He was so genuine and fun to be around. He listened to me and actually heard what I was saying."

"So go back and talk at him some more," Amy said.

"What do you mean?"

"So he's a prince incognito. He helped you take down wallpaper. He must be interested in you."

"You think so?" Elise remembered Wes's strong arms reaching over her head to tug the paper off the wall. He smelled of the sea and something exotic she couldn't name. Her nostrils flared as she tried to breathe in the aroma from her memory. "Should I just tell him that I know who he is then?"

"Sure."

"But he probably came here to hide. Maybe he'll be mad that I know," Elise said.

"Or not."

"Promise me you won't tell anyone."

Amy groaned. "It's not a secret anymore so I can't tell. Bonnie already did that, remember?" She pushed Elise toward the sidewalk. "Go talk to your prince, find out his story and kiss him."

"Amy!"

"If you don't, then I will. That's something to tell the grandchildren. Yummy."

"Okay, I'm going."

"I'll be waiting with this when you're ready." Amy held up her camera and waggled her eyebrows.

Elise thought about what Amy had said the rest of the day. By the time she drove to the B&B Saturday morning, she was ready to find the prince and confront him. She told herself that she wasn't thinking about the kissing part, but her heart didn't believe her.

CHAPTER SIX

When Elise reached the B&B just after eight that morning, she spent a few minutes lingering in the reception area and walked around outside, but there was no sign of the prince. She saw Maria, the housekeeper, working hard with her usual smile. Maria waved to her before heading into another room to clean.

When Bonnie came down the grand staircase, Elise hurried across the room and headed for the basement, flipping on lights as she went. She ducked under the caution tape that Bonnie had secured in the hallway and stood next to the last section of navy blue and paisley wallpaper. What if she'd missed her chance to talk to Wes? She should have been brave and talked to him yesterday, but the shock of the situation had turned her insides to mush. She refilled the unit with water and plugged in the steamer. The transformation of the room was what she tried to concentrate on as she waited for the steamer to heat up. She had just started to loosen the lower section of paper when someone cleared his throat behind her.

"Hey, I'm still here and I'm still taller than you. Can I help?" Wes asked. He looked like the boy next door with his tan cargo shorts and light green polo shirt. His black hair curled tightly along his temples and the light caught the dimple in his cheek. Absolutely gorgeous and completely untouchable. The prince of Riodan.

Elise's breath caught in her throat. She felt stupid that she hadn't recognized him. And in that moment, she knew why her embarrassment bothered her so much. She was attracted to Wes, she wanted to get to know him better. Even though she'd tried to deny it to herself because he was a tourist, her silly heart had pitter-pattered its way to the B&B every day since she'd first seen him. "Sure, this is the last wall so I wouldn't want you to miss your chance." Her words had an edge to them that she hadn't meant to come through.

Wes took a step back. "Um, are you okay?"

Elise set the steamer down and turned to face him. She rolled her shoulders back. "I didn't know that you were a prince and it caught me off guard."

His eyes widened and he glanced to either side of the basement. "Me?"

"Yes. You." Elise held up her phone and showed him a picture of himself decked out in a cream suit that probably cost more than her grandma's taxes for the past five years.

His shoulders slumped and he let out a sigh. "How did you find out? I've been so careful."

Elise snorted. "You're trying to hide while toting around armed security guards?"

Wes held up his hands. "Wait a minute. I don't have anyone guarding me. I escaped from the palace to get away from all of Titan's ridiculous schemes. My mother doesn't even know where I am."

Elise arched an eyebrow. "I'm trying to decide if that's your cover story or if you're living in some kind of alternate reality, because I saw your guards."

"No. No way." Wes shook his head. "Where?"

Either he was a really great actor or he didn't know about his security detail. "If I show you, will you tell me why you lied to me?"

"I never lied to you." Wes lifted his chin and Elise could see the challenge in his eyes.

"True. But what's that saying about how a lie of omission is still a lie?"

He pulled his bottom lip through his teeth. "I needed some space. You can understand that, right?"

Elise opened her mouth and then closed it before her words got her in trouble. Wes hadn't technically told her a lie and he wasn't acting different towards her, so maybe he was a nice guy even if he was a handsome, incredibly wealthy island prince. "Okay, follow me. Maybe we can catch them when they're not looking."

She touched Wes's arm as she walked past him and inclined her head up the back staircase. Wes followed and they went outside behind a large rhododendron bush. Elise surveyed the street for a moment. "There. That man over there is definitely one of your security guards." She pointed to a tall thin man leaning against a wrought iron fence across the street.

Wes squinted and took a step closer, ducking under the maple tree. "No. No way, that guy couldn't take my sister down. My guards are about three times that size."

"So, you're admitting you have a security detail here?"

"No, I'm talking about the guards that follow me around everywhere in Riodan."

Elise shook her head. "Poor little prince, so naïve. You fell for the oldest trick in the runaway child handbook."

Wes took a step back and snorted. "Please enlighten me."

She folded her arms across her chest and raised her chin. "Allow the four-year-old to think he has run away while keeping a close eye on him. Have a neighbor follow him, etc. etc. Let him escape and then figure out that it wasn't such a great idea after all."

"Did you just call me a four-year old?"

Elise lifted one shoulder and let it fall. Then she glanced out the front window. "That man is not a local. I don't know everyone in Echo Ridge by name, but I've never seen him here before."

"So, he's visiting the B&B, just like me," Wes said.

"Except he's not. He's not a tourist and he's not local. Pretty good guess that he's not American either."

Wes took a step back and rubbed his hand over his face. "I can't believe it." He looked up. "I bet that's his partner right over there." Elise leaned forward to see where he was pointing. A husky man with white-blond hair sat at the bus stop sipping a soda.

"Hmm, you might be right. I've never seen him either."

Wes groaned. "Titan is ruining my life." He set his mouth in a hard line and stepped away from the bush.

Elise grabbed his arm. "Wait, don't approach him. If he knows you know, then there might be some protocol in place for them to step up their security detail."

Wes hesitated and nodded. "You're right. Let's go back inside."

Elise jogged down the stairs as Wes took them two at a time. When they reached the basement, he ran his hand over his head and blew out a breath. "You must think I'm such a fool."

"No, actually. A bit cryptic yes, but I'm intrigued by you and I wanted to get to know you better. Now that your secret's out, the conversation won't have to be so one-sided."

Wesley arched an eyebrow. "I'll still be talking to you —or listening to you I guess."

Elise pushed his arm off the wall, knocking him off balance. "Hey, no fair using my weakness against me. Anyway, why don't we start over?" She held out her hand. "My name is Elise Gibson. I've lived in Echo Ridge most of my life with my Grandma Suzy and my younger brother, Mark. My dad's always been too busy for family so Gran has always been there for us. We live in a beautiful old house that my father was raised in and I work three jobs. Oh, and I love hyacinths."

Wes chuckled, but he shook her hand. "Hi, I'm Prince Weston Kai Montoya of Riodan. I have three brothers and two sisters. I've lived on the island my entire life, mostly within the palace sanctuary. I hate the paparazzi. I'm tired of women pretending to be interested in me when they're just looking for a way to Titan, so I escaped. Until thirty minutes ago, I thought my plan had worked and I've been thinking about the direction I want my life to go, but evidently my mother's plans trump all, as usual."

"Wow, that was impressive," Elise said.

"What?"

"You just spoke more than two sentences to me."

Wes gave her a full smile. "There's a first time for everything."

"That's the truth. Wait until I tell my friends that the prince of Riodan helped me take down wallpaper."

Wes grabbed her hand. "Please don't," he whispered.

Elise looked at his hand holding hers and at the fear in his eyes. He really did hate the paparazzi. "Don't worry. If there's any press around Echo Ridge, they are always hanging out at Ruby Mountain. If you stay away from there, you should be fine."

"But I'm serious. I'd like to keep my secret," Wes said. "Can you help me? How about this? We can take some pictures together and when I'm gone you can post them wherever you want."

Elise heard the desperation in his voice. "Wes, I'm not going to post anything if you don't want me to. Your secret's safe with me."

"Promise?" Wes asked with a hint of something in his voice that indicated he didn't believe her.

An image of Amy dangling her camera in front of Elise filled her mind. Should she tell Wes that Amy knew his secret too? If she did, he might be upset or worried enough to leave town before she even had a chance to get to know him. No, she'd just make sure that

Amy kept the secret too. Elise lifted up her hand and stuck out her pinky. She wiggled it and Wes gave her a strange look. She took his hand and straightened his pinky so she could loop hers around his finger. "It's a pinky promise. It means more than just a promise around here."

Wes smiled. "Pinky promise then."

He looked so relieved and suddenly more relaxed than he'd been before. Elise stared into his dark eyes. He still held her hand and he squeezed it gently. A slow river of heat pulsed through Elise's fingertips, up her arm and catapulted her heart into a staccato rhythm. "So, what now?" Elise whispered.

"More wallpaper?"

Elise laughed. "I think I'd better save a piece of this wallpaper. I could sell off scraps of it for years to come. Maybe buy Gran a new roof."

Wes chuckled. "We'd better get to work then."

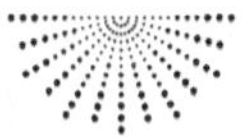

CHAPTER SEVEN

Wes returned to his room with a grin on his face. He'd spent an hour with Elise before she had to leave for her next job. He'd told her that he wanted to see her again. He hadn't had the courage to ask her on a date yet, because of all the problems that might bring up. Where could they go without someone recognizing him? But even the fear of the paparazzi discovering him couldn't keep him from wanting to see her again.

She'd distracted him from his anger and frustration with his family. Now that her bright smile and constant chatter was gone, Wes was left with the silence and the truth of who he was. It was still hard to believe that his mother had sent a security detail after him. Weston closed his eyes and thought about the interactions he'd had yesterday. The man with the white mustache—the one he'd seen leaving the B&B on his way back from his run.

Weston rubbed his forehead. How could he be so naïve as to think he could actually escape palace security? His anger rose again as he thought about all the hours he'd spent researching his project to build up the farming infrastructure of Riodan. Because of Titan's thoughtless posts on the internet, Wes had to leave his research site in order to think clearly. The past week he'd been able to analyze the data from two years of study growing different crops, measuring yields, and viability. With his sustainability project, he felt like he finally had a future in Riodan that excited him, that is until he was reminded that he would forever be under surveillance. Wes pulled out his phone and pushed the speed dial for number three.

"Weston, I didn't expect to hear from you so soon."

"You blew my cover!" he growled at his mother.

"Weston, I did it for your safety."

She hadn't even paused. Weston heard what she hadn't said. Maybe she expected him to notice sooner. Another of her games, probably. "Then why pretend that you were worried for me and didn't know where I was hiding?"

"Because I knew that you needed some time and space to figure things out. I'm sorry that I wasn't forthright, but your father would have sent the armed guard after you if I hadn't intervened. We've had security detail on all of our children since you were teenagers. How else could we keep Titan out of jail?"

Weston ground his teeth. "Inconceivable!"

"Darling, why don't you just go on pretending that you haven't noticed them and they'll do their jobs without interfering in your business. Although it seems like you might have a few admirers, so be careful."

"What? So you're spying on me too? Are they sending you footage or something?"

"A queen has a right to protect her lineage. That's all I'm saying."

"Inconceivable! I can't believe you would do this to me."

"You keep using that word. Is it American? I do not think it means what you think it means."

"Mother! I can't talk to you right now." Weston hung up on the queen of Riodan and promptly turned off his phone. His heart was pounding out of his chest and the tension radiating off his shoulders could've powered a small city—perhaps even Echo Ridge.

CHAPTER EIGHT

The rain moved in and decided to announce the official arrival of spring. On Tuesday, the fourth of April, Elise dashed into the house, the water dripping off her umbrella and coat. Her feet were wet. She'd have to remember to dig her rain boots out of the closet.

Piano music filtered from the front sitting room and Elise took a deep breath. Shedding her rain gear, she felt the stress of the day dripping away with the beautiful classical music her grandmother played. Growing up, Suzy had taught piano lessons to most of the youngsters in Echo Ridge at one time or another. Elise remembered many days coming home from school and listening to the piano while she ate her after-school snack and did her homework.

The past couple years Grandma had pared down her

roster of students to only five each week. Her back bothered her more now and it was hard to sit in a chair for hours tutoring students.

Elise walked into the front room and leaned against the door way. The grand piano was a deep cherry wood, still polished to a high sheen. Milo came every year to tune it, clean it, and make sure everything was in working order. He had stolen a piece of Elise's heart but that had changed to a valuable friendship. And because Elise was outspoken, she took a little credit in pushing timid Milo, the skilled musician, to voice his feelings for Britta the librarian. Elise wondered what Milo would think if she told him she'd taught a Riodanian prince how to remove wallpaper.

"Hello dear," Grandma said as she continued to play.

"It's good to hear you playing again," Elise said. "How are you feeling?"

"Better today. Since the rains came, my elbow stopped hurting." Grandma finished playing the piece by Liszt and turned to face Elise. "I was thinking that maybe I could take on more students again."

"Gran, we talked about that."

She held up her hand. "I know, but I saw the tax notice and we've got to do something."

Elise sighed. She looked upwards, following the lines of the high ceiling. She was about to tell her grandma that she'd take on more work when Elise noticed a dark spot where the ceiling met the wall. She leaned forward and squinted. "Oh, no."

"What is it?" Grandma stood and craned her neck to see what Elise was looking at.

"I've got to run up to the attic. We might have a leak."

"Oh, mercy. I hope not," Gran replied. "Take a flashlight."

Elise dashed through the kitchen and grabbed the flashlight off the windowsill. She climbed up two flights of stairs to the attic and kicked at the door. It was solid wood and had swelled along the bottom over the years so it was always stuck shut. The door came open with a pop and Elise allowed her eyes to adjust to the gloom. She could hear the rain pounding on the roof in a gentle, yet constant rhythm. She stood in the doorway listening, holding her breath. Shining the flashlight along the edges of the roof, Elise looked for signs of water damage. She walked closer to the corner of the attic, above the spot she'd seen in the front room downstairs. There—she heard a dripping sound, and it sounded worse than any soundtrack in a horror movie. Elise followed the noise and the beam of the flashlight illuminated a sparkle of water dripping from the roof. "Please, no," Elise whispered.

She dropped the flashlight to the ground and sunk to her knees. Elise closed her eyes and listened to the rain. She'd always loved the rain and the rainbows that came after the storm, streaking the sky with promise. Clenching her fists, Elise bowed her head and prayed, "Lord, I can't do this on my own. I need help. Gran needs help. I don't know how we're going to make it." The backs of her eyes burned with tears and she swallowed. "I'm doing the best I can. Please, can you send someone to help us?"

Elise knelt in the semi-darkness of the attic listening to the rain. Her thoughts were redirected to the fragile crocuses that were always the first to bloom in the spring. It was thrilling to catch a glimpse of the green poking through the melting snow announcing to the world that the earth would be reborn again. Elise felt peace wash over her. She didn't know how they'd solve this latest problem, but they would get through it.

CHAPTER NINE

Elise had done the best she could to remedy the leak by placing a tarp and buckets and tins under the dripping spots. Then she called around for recommendations for someone to come and look at the damage. She was referred to Redbuilt Construction. It was a new company and the secretary was full of sympathy for Elise's plight. She promised to send someone over first thing in the morning. Elise went to sleep that night with a prayer in her heart, clinging to the hope she'd felt earlier.

Wednesday morning the rain hadn't ceased and Elise went to work at Paisley's Petals holding her umbrella high. She ran home for lunch and on the way, the clouds parted and the sun came out, dotting the wet asphalt with shimmers of reflected light. Elise saw the Redbuilt truck in the driveway and scanned the roofline. She didn't see anyone, but then a guy walked around the side of the house. His hair was dark with the dripping rain, his company shirt soaking up the water. He wore carpenter jeans and kneepads and a heavy tool belt hung on his hips. He slipped a hammer into one of the loops and Elise noticed the way his bicep bulged along his shirt sleeve. As he approached, something about his gait was familiar. He was shorter than her prince, maybe five foot ten inches, but he was every bit as broad as Wes through his shoulders. And then he looked up and smiled at her. Elise's heart fell into her stomach.

Billy Redford. The high school quarterback that every girl had drooled over on Friday night games. Senior year he'd let his wavy hair grow out and Elise remembered seeing the dark blond curls trailing out from under his helmet. Elise and her friends didn't care about football, specifically. She kept her eye on Billy whether he had the ball or not. But Billy was off-limits. He always had a girlfriend. Usually the petite and perky cheerleaders, so she'd admired him from afar and when he left on a football scholarship to Syracuse she'd let her dreams of him fade with the passing years.

"Can't believe it decided to stop raining *after* I got on the roof." He approached, lifting his head toward the sky. "Hopefully we'll get a reprieve and I can get started on the repairs."

"Billy?"

"Yeah?" He studied her, his brows furrowing as if he was searching his memory for her face.

Elise held out her hand. "Elise Gibson. We went to high school together."

"Elise?" He stepped closer and his blue eyes sparkled. "It *is* you." He ignored her hand and pulled her into a hug. "I thought I'd heard you were still around. Nice to see a familiar face."

Billy Redford was hugging her. Brain. Engage. Now. Elise struggled to remember what he'd said. All she could feel was the strength of his arms around her. As he released her and took a step back, Elise found her voice. "I never really left. Are you back for good?"

Billy nodded. "I finished up my degree in construction management, worked my tail off for other people and last year decided to start my own company."

"Wait. This is your company?"

Billy grinned. "Yep."

Elise saw the connection now between his last name, Redford, and Redbuilt construction.

"That's impressive," Elise said. "So you build houses?"

"Right now I'm building up a name for myself so I'm mostly working on remodels and repairs but I'm going to start my first build this summer."

"Congratulations. Wow, it's so good to see you after all these years." She knew she was borderline gushing but Billy Redford was talking to her, acting like they'd been friends for forever.

"I know. It's almost our ten year reunion." Billy rubbed the back of his neck, his fingers brushing the ends of his short hair. Elise wondered if he was remembering his long, wavy hair from those years—she was.

"Don't remind me. I'm pretending that I'm still eighteen and deciding what to do with my life."

Billy chuckled. "Well, let me know how that goes since I think most of us are in the same boat."

She liked that he seemed to understand a little of what she felt—the something that bordered on restlessness she'd felt lately about her life and even Echo Ridge. Elise decided to change the subject. "So, you might be able to get started on the roof today? Is it bad?" Elise cringed before he answered because everything with repairs was always more than she wanted it to be.

Billy must have noticed the expression on her face. "Hold on, don't panic. I'm still assessing the damage, but well, I don't think it'll be that bad."

"But it's the roof," Elise said. "They aren't supposed to leak."

"And I was supposed to go on to be a football coach," Billy said. "Life is full of surprises. Why don't you let me handle this one?"

"What's that supposed to mean?"

Billy laughed and the sound sent shards of light

through the darkness in Elise's soul. She remembered his laugh. He'd been a happy kid and even though he was larger than life, she'd never seen him treat others poorly. He was cocky, but what high school quarterback wasn't? Elise joined in his laughter and it felt good.

"I'll get you a bid, but if this weather holds I'm going to get started today. Is that okay?"

"Sure, I'm just here for lunch, but then I have to get back to work." Elise nodded, but then hesitated, "Um, do you have an option for me to make payments if needed?"

Billy's face softened. "Of course, but try not to worry. It doesn't look too bad."

"Okay, I'll try." But she was already worrying because she didn't have the money to cover any extra expenses but she didn't want to confess her financial state to Billy right now. And they lived in Echo Ridge, New York. It was April and if they didn't get the roof fixed it would cause more damage that would add up to more expenses.

"I'll see you tomorrow then?" Billy asked.

"I'll try to swing by at lunch to check on things." Elise looked at her watch. "I'd better hurry."

Billy waved as Elise jogged up the front porch steps. Her heart pumped the good vibes Billy had just given her through her core. She shook her head. She wasn't in high school anymore, but with the way Billy looked now that wasn't a bad thing. The B&B would take up the rest of her work day and Elise was hoping she'd see Wes again, but as she drove toward Main Street, Elise wondered if she should stop daydreaming about a prince and pay attention to the real-life man who was climbing up on the roof of her one-hundred-and-twenty-year-old house.

Elise arrived early at the B&B Thursday to go over her expense sheets and project list. She tallied up the items and labor she'd figured into her bid and hoped that she could pull off this project and make the kind of profit she needed to help pay the taxes and fix the roof. Wes came down the stairs just as she was checking the walls to prep them for painting. "Man, this place is depressing. There's so much work still to do," she grumbled. "Carter, the owners' son, built a whole gazeebo for a wedding in like two weeks and I'm still down here plugging away.

"It's not that bad," Weston said.

Elise turned to him and then flourished her hand toward the chipped sheetrock and the grotesque green shag carpet, her eyes bulging.

Weston took a step back, chuckling. "So what's the next step?"

"The painters arrive tomorrow. I selected a warm gray color for the walls and a gray with brown undertones for the trim."

"Sort of boring," Wes said. "Why are Americans afraid of color?"

Elise held out the swatches of color she'd selected. "Too much color is distracting. It makes it hard to relax."

"I disagree. Color brings out creativity and soothes the emotions at the same time, but only if it's done right."

"Hmm, you may have a point there, your highness," Elise teased.

"I'm not trying to be overbearing with my opinions just because I'm a prince." Wes shook his head. "I don't make you feel that way, do I?"

"No, actually you don't." Elise looked into his eyes and he held her gaze.

"Good, because I wanted to ask you something." He took a step closer and Elise noticed the way he filled the space around her. His presence wasn't intimidating. He was a large man, all muscles and sinewy strength.

"Ask away."

"Could I take you out on a date?" Wes put one of his large hands on her arm. His skin was black against her pale, freckled forearms and Elise noted the contrast but at the same time felt connected to him. He was a foreign prince, larger than life, from a fairy-tale reinvented, but when he touched her, she felt like she was home.

"I'm—uh, yes, that would be fun."

"For a minute there, I thought you were going to say no." The cadence of his voice reminded Elise of the steel drums and calypso bands she loved. Everything about him was music, but it was a tune she'd never heard before.

"No, I was just wondering what a prince does on a date."

"How about going to one of those old movies they're showing downtown?" Wes asked. "I noticed the one for tonight is *Roman Holiday*."

"I think that'd be fitting considering we're redecorating the theater room. Maybe we'll get some inspiration."

"I'm sure of it."

Elise had the distinct feeling that Wes was talking about a different kind of inspiration than she'd been implying. Instead of trying to figure out what he meant, she concentrated on her work. "If I want to go on a date, I'd better get to work spackling these walls."

Wes furrowed his brow. "Spanking?"

Elise giggled. "I keep forgetting that your royal fingers haven't done much dirty work."

"Hey, I've done my share of work. Our family has a

lot of responsibilities on the island. The Montoyas have always valued agriculture, so we're one of the few islands in the Caribbean that is self-sufficient."

"Hmm, that is impressive. I'm trying to picture you working in the fields but my imagination is falling short." She grabbed the container of spackling compound and popped it open. She held it under Wes's nose so he could examine the creamy pink paste. "I take a dab of this and use a scraper and fill in the holes in the wall." She demonstrated how to fill a small nail hole with the paste. "When it dries, it will be white."

He nodded. "Kind of like wood putty. I used some of that in my woodworking classes. So do you have to fix all of the gouges in these walls?"

"Yep. The painter usually does this but we're working on a tight timeline so I told Bonnie I'd do the extra work. I need the money anyway."

"You're a hard worker. Maybe too hard?"

His question made Elise bristle. It seemed everyone was always telling her to relax and take it easy. She worked quickly filling in several holes and swiped off the excess putty before answering. "My grandma's house has a leak in the roof and the property taxes are past due, so yes, I do work too hard but I don't have another choice. I don't expect *you* of all people to understand."

"Hey, that didn't come out right. I wasn't trying to be condescending. Are all New Yorkers as sarcastic as you?" His voice had an edge to it. He sighed and continued before Elise could answer. "I actually know how to work and I had plenty of opportunities. Riodanian royalty is different. The people don't support us, we support the people."

"What do you mean?" Elise asked, contrite under Wes's rebuttal to her attack.

"How many islands do you know that are self-sufficient?" Wes asked.

Elise shrugged. "I'm not much of a world economist." She reached her arms around in a circle. "I'm surviving in my own little sphere."

"Some of your Hawaiian islands are totally reliant on imports. They produce very little to support the infrastructure of their island as far as basic necessities like food."

"I didn't know that," Elise admitted.

Wes scooped out a gob of spackling with his index finger and smoothed it over a couple nicks in the wall. Elise followed after with the scraper. "With four boys, my parents utilized the tutelage of the agronomists quite often. They sent us out into the fields to "study" at least once a day during the growing season. It never felt like study to me. It was fascinating. I loved working the land and learning about how it helped our country's economy." His eyes lit up as he spoke and Elise realized that he wasn't making it up.

"What kind of crops?"

"Sweet potatoes, corn, wheat, alfalfa, rice, sugar cane." He ticked off the crops on his fingers. "I could go on and on. My older brother Zac studied agronomy and has been working on producing natural growing techniques so that we don't have to use pesticides."

"I hate to admit it, but I didn't even know Riodan existed until your brother got in trouble with that cockfighting incident."

Wes groaned.

"Sorry, I shouldn't have brought that up. I know it's a sore subject with you. I'm really sorry about how your brother is acting."

"He's ruining everything we've worked so hard to create. Our country has always had lots of tourists, but since Titan's episodes last year, the tourism has gone up seventy-five percent. It's changing our island and I don't like it." Wes leaned against the wall. "It's tearing our family apart. My father is so angry all the time and my mom keeps talking about how Titan is not the crown prince anymore."

"I know it's not the same thing, but I do understand what it's like to have someone you love make bad decisions."

"You do?"

Elise put the lid back on the spackling compound and leaned against the wall next to Wes, her arm brushing his. "My dad dropped me and my brother off at my grandma's after my mom died. He didn't want to deal with us. It hurt." Elise put a hand over her heart. "It still hurts."

"I'm sorry. That's terrible."

"It was, and I wish it wasn't true, but I'm better off without him in my life. My grandma Suzy has given me all the love I could've hoped for and I like living in Echo Ridge. I just wish I could've had a chance to go to college like my little brother—but I didn't get a full-ride scholarship. I mean, I still could have gone, but Gran can't make it financially without me right now."

"That must be hard to be torn between doing two good things. What would you have studied?"

"Design," Elise answered automatically. "I had dreams of opening my own design studio. In a way, I've still done that I guess, it just looks a little different than my dream."

"Real life usually does." Wes turned to face her. "You're a stronger person than I thought when we first met."

Elise smiled and flexed her bicep. "Thanks. You're quite a bit more royal than I thought you were when we first met."

Wes rolled his eyes. "You gonna hold that over my head forever?"

"You mean the fact that you're a prince?" Elise teased.

"Yes, your highness." A thrill went through her middle when Wes said forever. It was just a saying, but what if him asking her out on a date was more than just a weekend fling or a vacation? What did he really mean when he said forever?

"I've got a few things to do before tonight. See you at six?" Wes asked.

"Sure. Thanks for your help."

As Wes walked out of the room, Elise wondered what he did during the hours of every long day when he wasn't helping her in the basement of the B&B. He'd mentioned agronomy and some projects, but it was probably difficult to enjoy Echo Ridge while he was trying to keep his identity hidden.

CHAPTER ELEVEN

es found it hard to focus on why he'd come to Echo Ridge in the first place when every other thought was filled with Elise Gibson. She was a breath of fresh air, with so much vibrant energy that he couldn't help but feel invigorated when he was around her. He'd finally worked up the nerve to ask her out on a date and his cheeks hurt from grinning every time he thought about picking her up tonight. He hadn't been out on a real date in over six months. He shuddered when he thought of his last date selling him out to the paparazzi. The photos were still circulating on the internet and Wes hated the fact that pieces of his life he wanted to forget were just a click away for anyone curious enough to type in the Montoya name.

His mother wouldn't approve of him taking an American out on a date. At least that was one place where Titan was following the rules—he only hung out with people in Riodan. With all the tourists flocking to the island, it was hard to tell who was a native. Part of Wes rebelled at the stringent rules and expectations. Maybe he'd never return to the island, but that thought was chased away by the project he'd poured his soul into. He couldn't turn his back on his island.

Wes worked on his laptop for the rest of the afternoon on the new crop schedule for the upcoming year. He'd left right after first planting—on the isle of Riodan they grew things year round, so they could plant months earlier than farmers in upstate New York. His major project for college was on developing community gardens where people could work together, harvest together, and share their excess with the other citizens of Riodan. His next venture was studying how families could be more self-sufficient by raising chickens and sheep. There was a poor sector of Riodan that Wes had high hopes for. With education and attention, these people could find improved living conditions. Titan openly shunned the poor of Riodan, calling them island scum. The thought usually made Wes angry, but today it gave him an idea.

He jotted down notes and then called his mother.

"I have a crazy idea."

"So you're speaking to me again?"

"Mother, I'm upset that you couldn't give me space,

but I understand. Thank you for caring about my safety and I'm sorry for the extra stress I caused."

His mother didn't say anything for a minute and he heard a sniff. "Weston, I love you. You are a good son. I want you to be happy. You belong in Riodan and I don't think you'll be happy away from your island."

"It's not my island anymore. Titan has made sure of that, but that's why I called. I have an idea."

"I'm listening."

CHAPTER TWELVE

When Elise pulled in to the driveway for lunch, she saw the Redbuilt truck and immediately scanned the rooftop for Billy. Her nerves tightened when she saw him climbing down a ladder. Hopefully the damage wasn't extensive to the roof. She got out of her car and walked toward him.

"At least the weather is holding out for you today," Elise said.

"I couldn't have asked for a better day. How about you?" Billy looked up at the sunshine peeking through the clouds and back at Elise.

"It's been a busy one, but things are coming along nicely at the B&B."

"Did you know that Carter is looking to take over the B&B when his parents retire next year?"

Carter Montgomery was a few years older than she

and Billy—a senior when they were sophomores. "Yeah, kind of a shocker when you think how goofy he was in high school," Elise said.

Billy ran his hand through his hair. It was cut short along the sides with a bit of a wave on top. His skin was already sporting a tan which Elise thought was impossible in the dreary springtime weather. "It's kind of crazy to think we've been out of school for eight years."

"I know," Elise said. "Some of our classmates have gone on to be so successful. I feel kind of lame. I never finished my college degree."

Billy shook his head and motioned toward the house. "Elise, you're where you should be. Your grandma loves you so much. You've sacrificed a lot for her and this house. That's successful in my book."

Elise blinked several times. "How did you know?"

"People talk, your Grandma Suzy, especially," Billy said. "She's so worried for you, trying to shoulder everything on your own."

Elise wasn't sure if she should feel embarrassed or grateful that Billy was aware of her struggles. She licked her lips.

Billy touched her arm. "I might have some good news for you. This roof repair is pretty minor. I think it'll only cost two-hundred, maybe two-fifty."

"What? Really?" Elise felt like a two-ton weight had suddenly been lifted from her shoulders.

"Sure, you've got some work to do inside to clean up, but I think together we can get this fixed pretty easily."

Elise looked over at the roof and then back at Billy, a smile spreading across her face. "That is such a relief."

"I agree. Maybe calls for a little celebration. Are you busy Friday? I wanted to take you to the tulip festival." Billy's stance was relaxed, but his right index finger twitched back and forth over his tool belt.

Elise hesitated for a second, trying to process her high school dream coming true. How strange that only a week ago, she would have been ecstatic about Billy's invite. But she was going out on a date tonight with the prince of Riodan and she wasn't sure if she should hope for a possibility with Wes or not. She swallowed. Billy was a good friend and he was fixing their roof. Maybe he really did just want to catch up as friends. Elise reminded herself that Wes was just passing the time while he took a break from his royal duties. The reality check made her squirm because a part of her hoped she was wrong. "I'd love to."

"Great. I hope to be done working on the roof by then so maybe we could walk around the festival and then grab something to eat. How early can I pick you up?"

"I could be ready by five, would that work?"

Billy grinned. "Perfect."

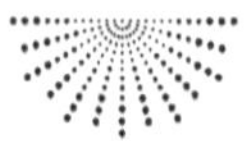

Wes drove his rental car to Elise's house, his palms sweating against the steering wheel. He felt almost as nervous as he had at age sixteen when the princess of Aruba had visited the palace and danced with him. He wanted things to go well tonight. Elise constantly surprised him with her witty remarks, blunt statements, and genuine beauty. With her dark brown hair and fair skin, she would be a contrast to most natives of Riodan.

She answered the door, dressed in a white and blue floral dress that skimmed her knees, showing off shapely legs. He pulled his eyes back to her face, where her emerald eyes were rimmed with dark mascara. "You look beautiful."

She smiled and reached out for his hand. "You look like a prince."

Wes took her hand, glancing down at the light gray suit pants he'd selected for the evening. His dark green sport coat was cut stylishly to enhance his build and he stood up straighter under Elise's admiring gaze.

"I'd like to introduce you to my Grandma Suzy. Is that okay?"

"Does she know my last name?" Wes whispered.

Elise shook her head and tugged on Wes's hand. He admired the house as they walked into the front room. It was old but well built, with strong beams, graceful arches, crown molding outlining the walls of the rooms. The flooring creaked and popped in a few places as he walked across the hallway. He noticed a beautiful grand piano in the corner. "Do you play?" he motioned toward the ivory keys, gleaming under the light of the piano lamp.

"I used to play more than I do now. My grandma teaches piano."

"Oh, she still teaches? How long has she been teaching?"

"Forty-three years and don't you dare try to guess my age." Grandma Suzy entered behind them. Her white hair was curled softly framing her round face. Her light blue eyes took him in quickly and Wes straightened and almost bowed before he remembered himself.

He held out his hand. "It's a pleasure to finally meet

you. I've heard a lot about you. I'm Weston, but you can call me Wes."

"Suzy Gibson. Thank you. I haven't heard anything about you. Elise likes to keep secrets."

Wes wasn't sure if his dark skin would hide the blush creeping up his skin. He coughed and used a trick from his royal training to re-center himself when someone was trying to throw him off guard. "Really? Elise talks nonstop when I'm around."

Suzy chuckled and her smile widened. She turned to Elise. "Ah, I see why you've been keeping him a secret. He's a keeper, isn't he?"

"Grandma!" Elise protested. "This is our first date. Wes is visiting Echo Ridge while working on some projects."

Grandma put her hand on his arm. "Well, I hope your research goes well. Elise knows everything about Echo Ridge. You couldn't have picked a better tour guide." She winked, exaggerating the moment.

"We'll see you later Gran. Have a good night." Elise took Wes's arm and steered him toward the front door.

"It was nice to meet you Suzy," Wes called over his shoulder as Elise dragged him away.

"Now that's what I call a man," Suzy said as they walked away.

"Grandma!" Elise quickened her step and Wes bit the inside of his cheek to keep from laughing.

Wes liked Elise's grandma. He also liked the red spots on Elise's cheeks and the way her lip jutted out as she concentrated on getting him away from her grandma.

Elise could feel silent laughs vibrating Wes's arm as they stepped outside. "Sorry, I should've warned you."

"That you are exactly like your grandma?" Wes asked. "She's sweet. It's refreshing to be around someone who isn't afraid of honesty."

"Well, that's me and Gran."

"I know." He winked as he opened her door.

They drove to The Silver Screen theater and Elise smiled when she saw the old movie posters for *Roman Holiday*. Audrey Hepburn was a timeless beauty and Gregory Peck was every woman's dream man in the 1950s when the film was first released.

The lobby smelled like popcorn and roasted peanuts and Wes stood in line to order a jumbo bucket of popcorn. "Do you like butter on your popcorn?"

"Yep and extra salt."

"Anybody want a peanut?" a man called over the counter. "Hot roasted peanuts for your true love tonight."

Elise blushed. "I think I'm good with the popcorn."

Wes guided her down the hallway and helped her

into one of the red plush velvet chairs and sat beside her. His large frame filled the seat and he sat more than a head taller than Elise. As the movie started, he put his arm around her. "I hope you don't mind that I'm not very subtle."

She giggled.

"You smell wonderful," he whispered in her ear and it sent chills down her arms. He pulled her close to him and she leaned toward him and sniffed.

"You smell like an island getaway."

"Nah, probably more like popcorn."

They flirted with each other until Audrey Hepburn started talking.

During the movie, Elise had a heightened awareness of Wes. After a while, he moved his arm from around her and held her hand. They shared popcorn and junior mints and Elise felt more relaxed than she'd been in weeks. She got lost in the story of Princess Anya and Joe but she noticed every time Wes rubbed his thumb over the top of her hand.

When the final credits rolled, Elise didn't want to move. She wanted to sit close to Wes and feel his arm around her. "I don't really like the ending to that movie," she whispered.

Wes nodded. "I had forgotten. I don't like it either—reminds me too much of my life." He stood and helped her up.

His words rang in Elise's ears. *Roman Holiday* was a sad movie because two people fell in love but couldn't be together. The princess could not follow her heart with the commoner. Elise didn't like the similarities to her current situation. But Wes offered her his arm as they walked out of the theater and Elise decided she would forget the ending of the movie. Wes helped her into the car. "So what do people do in Echo Ridge after watching classic films?"

"Pretend that real life is better than the movies?" Elise offered.

"Well, if you'd like to visit Riodan sometime, I might be able to convince you of that."

Elise's heart cartwheeled in her chest. "How would you do that?"

"White sand beaches. Water so clear you don't need snorkeling gear. Sunsets that make you fall in love. We have a little bit of everything." Wes drove toward her house as he spoke.

"That sounds like a fairy tale," Elise said, voicing her constant fear that she was in some kind of alternate reality instead of in a car having a normal conversation with a prince.

"Does that mean I'm your prince charming?" The dimple in his cheek deepened as he smiled.

"No way," Elise said. Wes frowned and his shoulders

slumped, but Elise reached over and squeezed his bicep. "You're much better looking than him."

Wes straightened and Elise laughed when his dimple reappeared. "Thanks." He glanced at her. "You remind me of Snow White though with your dark hair and your red lipstick." He faced the road again.

"Thank you." Elise touched a finger to her lips. He'd noticed her lipstick which meant he'd been looking at her mouth. Had he been thinking about what it might be like to kiss? Before she could dwell on that thought too long, Wes pulled into her driveway and helped her out of the car. He walked her up the front steps and they stood just outside the arc of the old porch light.

"I had a great time tonight. Can we do this again sometime?" Wes asked.

"That depends on if you'll still be here or not," Elise replied.

Wes took a step closer to her, cupping her elbows with his hands. "I'm not going anywhere soon. I have too much work to do."

"What kind of work?" His hands were warm on her skin, little goosebumps popped up on her arms.

"A project I've been researching. I won't bore you with the details."

"Going all cryptic again?" Elise folded her arms.

"No, it's more work for my sustainable self-sufficiency project on the island." He didn't drop his hands;

instead he threaded them around her middle. Elise struggled to remember what they'd been talking about because she felt like he was testing her.

"Well that sounds like quite a mouthful. Why is it boring?"

He flashed his mega-watt smile and Elise relaxed her stance and put a hand on his chest. "Come on. Bore me. I dare you."

The dimple in his cheek deepened as he chuckled. "I'm trying to work with the disadvantaged sectors of Riodan to educate the people on how to grow their own food. A full belly is the gateway to knowledge. If people can look beyond their next meal, they can focus energy on learning how to better themselves and their family."

Elise thought about what he'd said. "I agree."

"You do?" Wes tilted his head, studying her for a reaction.

"Of course. Why do you think the free breakfast and lunch program in our schools has been so successful?"

"Wait, your government pays to feed the children at school?"

"Yes," Elise said. "Every community is different, but a child should never go hungry in America. That isn't the case, of course, but I ate free lunch during all my school years. It wasn't Gran's food, but it was one less worry for her."

"Fascinating."

"What? Me? Why, thank you." She patted his chest.

"Yes, actually. You just grasped my idea in a couple sentences and then gave me inspiration to continue my project." He lowered his head, his eyes flicking to her lips. His arms tightened around her waist and Elise raised her chin slightly as he came closer. The porch light flickered and a gust of wind swept across the porch, catching the screen door. It banged against the side of the house and Elise jumped, moving just enough that Wes brushed a kiss against her cheek before releasing her.

"Mercedes is out tonight causing trouble," Wes said.

"Who?"

"She's a Riodanian legend. She was one of the first princesses betrothed to a Montoya. On the eve before their marriage, her prince's ship caught on the coral reef and sunk in a storm. He was never found, so Mercedes roams the earth on the winds of a storm looking for her true love."

"That's intriguing," Elise said. Thunder rumbled in the distance and she smelled the rain before she saw it.

"You'd better hurry before you get caught in the storm. I'll be at the B&B tomorrow morning."

Wes looked like he wanted to stay but a flash of lightening cracked open the sky and the rain began to fall in earnest. He turned to go, holding onto the tips of her fingers, slowly releasing them from his grasp. "Tomorrow."

Elise stood on the porch inhaling the spring rain and trying to make sense of what had just happened to her heart. She was pretty sure Weston Montoya had taken it with him.

CHAPTER FOURTEEN

The next morning, the ground was wet with a drizzle of rain that continued but Elise and her Gran were able to enjoy the earth's life blood because Billy had repaired the roof and no errant drops of rain were sneaking into their home. Billy had insisted that they wait to pay him until they received the bill because it was easier for their record keeping, but Elise figured it was a kindness he'd extended to them and she had graciously accepted his direction. Her stomach flipped when she remembered that she had agreed to go on a date with Billy tonight. She bit her bottom lip, wondering if it was a good idea after the date she'd had with Wes. But all she had to do was remember the plot-line of *Roman Holiday* and how things had turned out for the princess. She shook her head. She wouldn't burn any bridges just yet.

She dressed carefully in her favorite pair of skinny jeans and a yellow blouse that contrasted well with her dark hair. She'd take an old button-up shirt to work in, but she wanted to look good for Wes. Braiding her hair to the side, she tucked a loose curl behind her ear and grabbed her purse from the side table. Her hand was on the doorknob when someone knocked. Elise jumped back, startled from her thoughts of when she would see Wes again and how she would feel spending time with Billy. She opened the door and saw a man that caused dread to curl around her legs, leaving her rooted in place.

"Hello, I'm Mr. Decker with the county assessor's office." He extended his hand and Elise reached out slowly, knowing that he'd have a dead fish grip before she even touched his perfectly manicured fingers.

"Elise Gibson, please come in."

"Thank you. Is Suzette home?" He stepped inside, clutching the leather briefcase at his side.

"Yes, she's in the living room. I'm her granddaughter, is there anything I can help you with?" Elise wanted to spare her Grandma this conversation if she could.

"I'd like to speak with her, if possible."

"Sure, hang on a minute." Elise left him standing there in his perfectly pressed suit, holding his briefcase with overdue tax notices. Gran was sitting in her favorite lounge chair, reading the paper.

"Gran, there's a man here from the assessor's office. I'm sure it's about the property taxes."

"Oh, heavens. Well, we'd better handle this one way or another." She rose stiffly and rolled her shoulders back, but Elise noticed that her back wasn't as straight as it used to be.

"I'll help you Gran." She slipped her arm through Gran's and they made their way to the front of the house.

Gran walked right up to Mr. Decker and smiled. "Well, I'm sure you're here to scold me about my overdue property taxes, but I don't need any scolding or threatening. I've paid what I could thus far and I'll pay the rest as soon as I have the funds to do so."

Mr. Decker cleared his throat. "Uh, Mrs. Gibson, I'm here as a courtesy to inform you that your taxes are two-hundred and sixty days late."

"Well not all of them. Don't I get any credit for what I've paid?" Gran put her hand on her hip.

"Yes, of course, but I need to return to the office with reassurance that you will have these taxes paid within ten days. Otherwise—"

"Uh-uh." Gran shook her finger in Mr. Decker's face. "No threats. You return to your little office and tell them that you spoke with me. I've lived seventy-two years and always made my payments on time. I'm certain that the county could help me. It's no peachy dream to get old.

I'm tired a lot more and I can't work like I used to. This old house is falling apart around us and Elise works three jobs to keep up with everything."

"I understand that, Mrs. Gibson," Mr. Decker said. He pulled out an envelope and handed it to her.

"No, I highly doubt that you understand, but I've said too much and my heart is racing. I need to lie down." Gran snatched the letter out of his hand.

"I'll give a full report and see what I can do," Mr. Decker replied. "And Mrs. Gibson?"

"Yes?" Gran gave him a withering stare.

"Get some rest. If you haven't got your health, then you haven't got anything."

"You're a dear." Granny patted his cheek. "Now go on and ruin someone else's day."

"I'll see myself out." Mr. Decker retreated quickly and Elise laughed until she snorted.

"Gran, I love you." She hugged Suzy. "We'll figure this out. I'm sure of it."

Gran opened the letter and Elise bit her lip to keep from saying anything. The total was still $6,385.00 with a large red stamp PAST DUE. A late fee of one-hundred-fifty dollars had been tacked on and if they didn't pay within ten days, the county would have grounds to put a tax lien on their property. That path could lead to foreclosure. Elise suddenly felt very tired.

"We'll never survive," she moaned.

"Nonsense," Gran said. "You're only saying that because no one ever has in the face of someone like Mr. Decker. We'll get through just like we always have."

Elise gave Gran a hug and hurried out the door before the tears broke through her carefully constructed dam. She'd planned to run a couple errands, but found herself driving directly to the B&B. She entered through the front door and stood in the hallway thinking about how much she wished she could climb the stairs and knock on Wes's door, unload her problems, and get on with her day. She covered her mouth as reality hit her full force. Wes was a prince—a very wealthy prince. Elise couldn't complain to him about how her financial troubles just kept getting worse because he might think she was just another gold digger out for his fame and fortune. She wasn't that. She was a Gibson and her family knew how to work hard and keep their heads above water. That was another of Gran's sayings that came in with a close second to, "Keep your chin up."

Elise drew in a ragged breath and raised her chin a notch. Her eyes betrayed her as a tear escaped, trailing down her cheek. The late fee on the property taxes was almost equal to what the repair on the roof would be. Every time Elise thought she was getting ahead, the bills came after her with a vengeance, knocking her down, stealing her joy, enslaving her in their chains. With a shake of her head, Elise rolled her shoulders back. She wouldn't get any further ahead by standing there feeling sorry for herself. The back door opened with a squeak and it moved Elise into action. She swiped a hand across her cheek and turned to dash down the stairs, instead she ran right into the arms of the very man she'd been wishing for.

"Whoa, good morning," Wes said as he pulled her close into his chest that was damp with sweat. He was all man and definitely doing something to her brain, because even his perspiration smelled tropical. Elise hugged him and then pulled back, her chin trembling.

"Hi, I was just going to get started. I, uh—." Now her lip was trembling and she knew she was no match for the waterworks that were pressing against her composure. "Can I talk to you in a few minutes? I've got one thing to do first." She didn't wait for an answer. Moving past him, she bounded down the stairs, her cheeks wet with tears by the time she hit the bottom step.

She flipped on the light and sank against the wall Wes had helped her spackle for painting. The gray was perfect for the basement and already the theater room looked a thousand times better than it did before. Elise's shoulders shook as a sob broke loose. She kept seeing Mr. Decker's stern expression and the way her Gran tried to act upbeat but her hands had shook anyway. Bowing her head over her knees, Elise whispered a silent prayer through her tears. She asked for mercy and help to get her emotions under control so she could work and hopefully talk to Wes without breaking down. Another sob shuddered through her body and she tried to suck in air, but even that was hard to do.

"Hey, what happened?" She felt a hand on her back and then Wes was sitting next to her on the floor. His presence unleashed a waterfall of tears and Elise kept her head down as thoughts raced through her head. How could she explain her problems to Wes? She shook her head.

"Is it something I did?" Wes asked.

"No." Elise turned her head to face him and her eyes widened when she saw the apprehension there. Wes cared about her. He must or he wouldn't be worried that he'd done something to cause her tears. She wiped her face on her shirt, thinking that she was probably the least glamorous girl Wes had ever spent time with.

"I'm sorry you're hurting. I'd like to listen if you want to tell me what's bothering you. I might not be able to help, but I'm pretty awesome, so you should try me."

Elise smiled and reached her hand out to squeeze his. "I'll be okay. Sometimes life just seems impossible, you know?"

He nodded. "I get that, but this," he motioned to her, "seems like more. . . like something very specific to get you crying like this."

Her throat was dry and she swallowed a couple times and sat up. "You're right."

Wes put his arm around her and gave her a side hug. Then he took her hand and squeezed it gently. They sat there for a moment, neither speaking and Elise felt the weight on her chest lift. Maybe she would be okay and maybe she should share her worries with Wes. He'd surprised her so far with the level of understanding of normal life he grasped even though he'd grown up in a tropical palace. "My grandma has lived in that house since she was a little girl so it was paid off sixty years ago, but every year the property taxes are more than the year before. This year we had some plumbing issues and other emergencies that drained our funds. I thought I'd be able to come up with enough to cover the taxes but then we got a leak in the roof."

"So in your country, the elderly don't receive support to live in the homes they've owned their whole life?"

"No, I mean, are you saying in Riodan they don't have property taxes?"

"We handle it differently. The property taxes must stay at the same rate they were when the owner turned sixty years of age. When the deed of ownership changes hands, then the tax increase is applied."

Elise leaned her head back against the wall. "That is so smart. Several of Gran's friends had to sell their homes when they got older because their fixed income couldn't support the tax hikes every year."

"How much do you owe?" Wes asked.

"No, that's not important." Elise shook her head. "Thank you for listening to me. I feel better now. I'm ready to get to work."

"It's important to me," Wes replied. "Maybe I could help you?"

Elise pressed her lips together, staring up at the ceiling. If she did confide in Wes, he would definitely help her. She knew him well enough now to understand what kind of person he was. But it might plant doubts in his mind about her true motives and she wasn't willing to risk that. She leaned forward and put her hand on Wes's arm. "You've helped me because you really listened. Thank you. Now, what do you have planned for your day?"

Wes stood and pulled her up into his chest. He hesitated before answering, probably deciding whether to press the issue or not. "A shower and then I'm meeting with a few people concerning my self-sufficiency project. Are you busy later?"

Elise almost said no before she remembered her date with Billy. It was strange now, standing in front of Wes how she was right back to hoping for the impossible with the prince of Riodan. "I am tonight, sorry."

The corner of his right eye twitched. "How about Saturday night then?"

She nodded. "That would be great."

"Can I take you to dinner?"

"That sounds even better."

"Where's your favorite?"

"The Overlook restaurant has a great selection, but maybe you'd like something more low-profile." Elise tapped her chin. "Let's see there's that nice restaurant by the resort, but maybe too crowded?"

"Oh, The Stone Hearth Lodge? That looked tasty," Wes said. "But yeah, I've been trying to steer clear of that area. What are you in the mood for?"

"Hmm, I'm not sure. What do they eat in Riodan anyway?"

"I'm missing the food that's for sure." Wes rubbed his stomach. "We eat a lot of fish, rice, artisan breads with native herbs from the island. Our chef makes a papaya sauce with noodles and Lionfish that I hate to miss and his grouper steaks are mouth-watering."

"That sounds interesting and delicious," Elise said. "I think you'll like the restaurants here too. Different fish —same ocean, but our seafood is pretty good."

"Your logic cracks me up."

"I'm glad you find me so amusing and I'd love to entertain you all day, but I'd better get to work."

"Don't work too hard, okay? Save some time to play."

Wes smiled at her and it made her heart hit several staccato beats in a row.

"I might try that someday."

"Okay, hopefully I'll see you before tomorrow night. If not, I'll pick you up at six."

"Sure, and Wes?"

"Yeah?"

"Thanks for listening."

He touched her fingertips before walking down the hallway. Elise waited until she heard his footsteps on the stairs before letting a girl squeal escape. She had another date with a prince. Even though she vowed not to get swept away by promises of a love that could never be, Elise felt the warmth of Wes's arms around her the rest of the day.

CHAPTER FIFTEEN

Wes went up to his room and showered. He glanced out the window, but he couldn't spot his security guards. They were there though. He'd tried a couple times to ditch them and thought he was successful only to see them around the next corner. They were good, maybe even better than his guards in Riodan. Wes grinned, but he wasn't thinking about the security detail anymore. He was picturing a beautiful woman with dark curly hair, a heart-shaped mouth, and an intoxicating scent of flowers that had him mesmerized. He couldn't get enough of her.

Elise was different from any woman he'd ever known. He wanted to be with her, but he wasn't sure how that was possible. He felt like a fish wanting to live on dry land, every breath felt like it was counting down to an impossible fate. Seeing her so upset had broken through the barriers he'd put up against relationships. Elise was like a butterfly, flitting with happiness from one flower to the next spreading sunshine and she was the only reason he was enjoying his stay in Echo Ridge.

She didn't want to tell him about her problems with finances and now as he stared at the royal crest imprinted on his ring, diamonds and emeralds dotting the band, he understood. She was afraid to tell him because she knew that gold diggers followed him everywhere. Wes ran a hand over his clean-shaven face as another realization struck him. Elise hadn't asked him for help and she purposely hadn't told him the amount due on her property taxes. Wes smiled. He had a few appointments for skype chats later, but now he needed to take a little drive.

He moved carefully through the B&B, trying to avoid anyone who might see him leaving. It was fine if his security detail followed him, but he didn't want Elise to know where he was going. It took a few minutes, but thanks to the GPS on his phone, Wes found the address for the county assessor's office. The red brick building housing the county offices looked ancient, with newer steel and glass buildings surrounding it. He wasn't sure if his plan would work, but he was going to try his very best.

The heavy wooden door slid across the striped brown and green carpet and Wes stepped inside a tiny front office. The secretary had her black hair braided intricately and she wore glasses with large gold frames that stood out against her dark skin.

"May I help you," she asked, looking him over carefully.

Wes hoped that she wouldn't recognize him. "Yes, I'd like to pay a property tax bill."

"What's the name on the account?"

"Suzette Gibson."

The secretary frowned. "Well, I'm pretty sure that's not you."

"No, but I would like to pay her bill. I understand that her taxes are overdue and I'd like to pay the entire bill. How much is it?"

The secretary huffed and typed on her computer. She scrolled down the page and her eyes widened. "$6,385.00. That's with the late fee added in." She looked at him, probably expecting him to blanch at the total. He didn't even flinch, but he was angry that such a paltry sum had the ability to steal the smile from Elise's face when Titan probably spent fifty-thousand dollars on his club parties every night.

"Is it possible for me to pay the bill for this year and the next ten years?" Wes asked.

The woman gaped at him. "But that would be. . ." she reached for her calculator.

"Almost sixty-thousand dollars," Wes supplied. It would hardly make a dent in his bank account. He'd done very well in college and he continued to work with the agronomy program for two more years after he'd graduated. He'd saved every paycheck. He had access to another checking account with a monthly stipend from his parents, but he wanted to do this for Elise and her Grandma with his own hard-earned money.

"We do take credit cards, but are you sure you want to do this?" the woman asked.

"Absolutely sure and I'd like this to be a surprise." Wes pulled out his debit card and slid it across the counter. "That'll run as a debit."

The woman's hands trembled as she ran the card and waited while he input his pin code. When she gave him the receipt, Wes smiled and thanked her. He tucked the receipt into his pocket, wishing he could go and tell Elise the good news right now. But he'd have to tread carefully and find a way to tell her later what he'd done and why he'd done it.

His parents had raised their children to think outside themselves and find ways to serve others, but that was hard to do inside the palace walls. Wes had done work on foundations and group efforts. They'd had plenty of service missions and opportunities, but Wes hadn't really understood how it felt to help an individual until that moment. He needed Elise because she'd given him a priceless lens through which to view the world. Tomorrow he wanted to tell her how she made him feel, and hopefully she would feel the same way.

CHAPTER SIXTEEN

The theater room in the B&B was starting to resemble the picture in Elise's head. A framed poster of *Gone with the Wind*, *Breakfast at Tiffany's*, *An Affair to Remember*, and *Sabrina* were artfully displayed on the large wall kitty corner from the huge flat screen TV. She had hung tin plates that were decorated with swirly designs and painted in turquoise, coral, and lime green in between each photo. There was a place prepared for a popcorn stand so that when someone entered the basement from the main staircase they would feel like they had arrived at a personal movie theater. Elise stood back, ticking off the things she needed to do to finish up the room.

"Well, this is coming together nicely," Bonnie said from behind her. "You've done great work Elise. "I just love the colors and those posters!"

"Thank you." Elise beamed. "It's been a fun project. I still have a lot of little touches, but I think we'll be ready on schedule."

"I've noticed you spending a lot of time with that prince," Bonnie ventured.

Elise bit her lower lip and waited a beat to answer. "He's quite friendly. I would have never guessed he was a prince if you hadn't told me."

"Yes, I've spoken with him a few times but I didn't let on that I knew his secret." Bonnie put her hand to the side of her mouth and whispered. "But those guards of his could take a few lessons in being covert. They stand around like lamp posts."

Elise leaned forward. "Well, I think it's great of you to keep his secret because he doesn't want anyone to know that he's here." She was driving her point home, hoping that it wasn't too little, too late.

Bonnie straightened. "Of course. My guests are the top priority and I do my best to know their business so I can keep it from others."

Elise had to swallow the spurt of laughter that threatened to bubble up at Bonnie's twisted justification for a die-hard busybody. "I think he's under a lot of pressure because of what his brother has done."

"That's for sure. His older brother is no good," Bonnie said. "The media has turned on him. His poor mother. My Carter would never—well, he's such a good man. And he's still single." She wiggled her eyebrows.

Elise nodded. "Yes, well, I'm off to Paisley's. I'll be back tomorrow."

Bonnie didn't blink at Elise avoiding the subject of dating Carter. "Thanks. You're a good girl. We're lucky to have your talent."

"Thanks, Bonnie." Elise hugged her. "That means a lot."

The three hours she put in at the floral shop felt like ten minutes because Elise was so busy and her mind was preoccupied with thoughts of her dates with Billy and Wes.

"You're quiet today," Paisley Scott said as she swept up remnants of rose petals. "But I'm sure it's anything but quiet inside your head."

Elise smiled. Paisley was about five years older than her and she was married with two kids. Every time Elise came to work, Paisley had her light brown hair pulled back into a long braid and she greeted everyone with a genuine smile. Elise liked Paisley and the delightful flower shop she'd opened in Echo Ridge two years ago. Space was a premium in the hundred-year-old building and Paisley kept hoping that she could expand, but for now it was just the right size for them to work comfortably and fill orders. "You're right. There's lots going on up here, but it's mostly boring stuff. Figuring out how to pay taxes and bills."

"Mostly boring huh?" Paisley hinted that she wasn't buying Elise's explanation.

Elise waved a bit of greenery at her. "I'm having a moment here with this order and I'm almost finished, so no badgering."

"Okay, okay, I can wait." Paisley smiled and swept toward the back of the shop.

Elise kept working until she finished with the beautiful display of white tulips with lily of the valley and grape hyacinths. She didn't want to voice the confusion in her head, but Paisley was a good listener. Elise pressed her lips together, itching with too many secrets. Using a polishing cloth, she rubbed the glass and adjusted a few more leaves. "This one is ready to go, and so am I." Elise set the arrangement on the counter.

"See you next week," Paisley said.

Elise waved and hurried out to her car. She smiled all the way home, feeling exactly opposite of how she'd felt when she left that morning. Gran was in the middle of a piano lesson, so Elise dashed up the stairs and changed into her favorite black leggings and a silky magenta dress shirt edged with cream lace. She put on a chunky multi-colored bead necklace and matching bracelet and earrings. The jumbo curling iron she loved made it easy to add soft curls to her dark hair. She reached for her red lipstick and at the last second chose a shimmery lip gloss, reserving the red for another night. She heard a pickup drive up and gave herself one final check in the mirror. She smiled. Billy might not have noticed her in high school, but he'd notice her tonight. She glanced out the window and saw the Redbuilt logo on his white truck. Since he'd already talked to Grandma when he worked on the roof, Elise decided to spare herself some mortification and meet him on the porch. Gran was still in the middle of piano lessons, after all. She stepped out from the front door as Billy was coming up the walk.

"Hey, beautiful," Billy said as he climbed the steps.

Elise smiled and ducked her head. "Thank you. I like your shirt." Billy was dressed in a blue and brown striped button-up shirt. He managed to look casual, yet classy at the same time in his stonewashed jeans that fit snug in all the right places.

Billy leaned in close, brushing a kiss to her cheek. Elise turned in surprise and they were face to face with her heart tap-dancing in her chest. Billy hesitated, his eyes flicking to her lips, and then he straightened, inter-lacing his fingers with hers. "Ready?"

"Sure am." Elise's voice sounded breathy in her ears. One night with the prince of Riodan and another with the prince of Echo Ridge High. She could get used to this. They chatted on the way to the lake and Elise felt like she'd slipped back a few years as they remembered friends from high school and updated each other on life.

As they walked around Chickadee Lake, Elise was excited about all the varieties of tulips. Billy held her hand and pretended to be interested in the flowers, but Elise kept catching him watching her. "Oh, look pink hyacinths!" She crouched down, pulling Billy with her. "You have to smell them. There's nothing like a fresh hyacinth. Perfumes don't do them justice." She sniffed and sighed. Billy leaned forward, humoring her to smell the flowers.

"You haven't changed much since high school. You're still the happy hummingbird I remember." Billy chuckled when Elise turned to him with eyebrows raised.

"I didn't think you really knew who I was in high school," Elise ventured.

"Of course I knew you," Billy replied. "My sister took piano lessons from your grandma. She teaches now in Albany. We love your family."

"Thank you." Elise appreciated his comment, but it didn't really show that he knew her.

"You always played beautifully, too. Do you still play?" Billy must have read her thoughts. Very few people knew that she played the piano because she hated playing in front of others.

"I was never that good, but once in a while I sit down and humor my grandma."

"So what do you do now?" Billy asked.

"A little bit of everything," Elise replied. "I work at Paisley's Petals part-time and I do designing and decorating whenever I can. I'm redecorating the theater room at the B&B. You should have seen the hideous navy blue wallpaper that I had to remove. Wes—I mean the pink in the design reminded me of Pepto Bismol." She'd almost slipped and mentioned Wes while on a date with another man. What was wrong with her? Billy Redford was taking her on a date. This was real. A prince from Riodan was the stuff of fantasies and she couldn't ignore the thought that she didn't really have a chance with Wes. Billy was here in Echo Ridge to stay.

"That's great. You seem happy. I'm glad you're doing something you love."

"You too. I'm impressed with you and your business. That's quite an accomplishment."

Billy's chest swelled with pride. "Thanks. I'm glad you think so."

"Thanks again for bringing me here. It's nice to stop and enjoy life for a few minutes."

"My pleasure," he said.

They drove to the Stone Hearth Lodge at the Ruby Mountain Resort and Billy walked around and opened her door for her. He took her hand and kept her close to his side as they entered the dimly lit restaurant. Elise recognized one of the waitresses as Lacey Johnson, the girl from California who'd moved to Echo Ridge a few years after Elise. Lacey waved and waggled her eyebrows in the direction of Billy, which made Elise blush. It was another reminder of how quickly word could spread in their small town. Lacey wouldn't say anything, but someone else at the restaurant might, and Elise wasn't sure how she felt about that. She mentally shrugged off her worries and determined to enjoy the date without over-analyzing Billy, the prince, or her uncertain future.

Over steak and potatoes, they reminisced about their childhood in Echo Ridge. Elise laughed at the things that Billy remembered, like the time she fell off the stage in drama class and was caught by one of the shyest boys at Echo Ridge. Rodrigo had blushed ten shades of red and checked out of the class.

Billy laughed, holding his sides. "Stop, Laney, you're killing me."

Elise stopped laughing and looked at the table. "It's Elise."

"What?" Billy leaned forward.

"My name is Elise, you called me Laney."

Billy flushed and put his head in his hand. "Oh gosh, I'm sorry. I don't know how that happened. I haven't thought of her in years."

Laney was the head cheerleader, blond, and extremely perky. Just like Billy had described Elise earlier … "Well, we were talking about high school." Elise shrugged.

Billy reached across the table and grabbed her hand before she could pull it back. "Elise, I promise she's not on my mind."

Elise stared at his fingers covering hers. "So whatever happened to Laney? Everyone thought you two would get married right out of high school and then I heard she married some guy from Kentucky."

"Yeah, that was rough. She met some guy that summer and followed him to another school. End of story."

"I'm sorry." Elise wasn't sure what else to say. It felt weird that Billy had called her the name of his ex-girlfriend. Was she just some proxy for him here in Echo Ridge? Maybe Billy wanted to be with her because she was familiar. Maybe she reminded him of everything he couldn't have when Laney left.

"I'm not sorry. My life would be completely different now. Laney never wanted to live in Echo Ridge. I love it here." Billy squeezed Elise's hand and smiled at her. "It took me a while to figure out where I was supposed to be. I think God wanted me here."

"Me too," Elise said. She meant that God wanted her in Echo Ridge too, but the way Billy sat up straighter, she realized he'd taken it that she agreed that he should be in Echo Ridge and maybe read more into the statement than she'd meant. Her attention strayed to Wes and her stomach did the little mamba dance it did every time she thought of him. Then the reality devil on her shoulder chimed in with the reminder that fairy tales don't happen in real life. Billy was here in Echo Ridge to stay while Wes was being pulled back to an island in the middle of the ocean. She turned and smiled at Billy. This was just a first date, but by the look on Billy's face there would probably be a second invitation coming soon.

They finished their meal, with the moment of awkwardness fading as they talked and laughed. Billy told her more about his construction company and Elise shared a few of her dreams for designing full-time. Billy took her home afterwards and walked her to the front door, still holding her hand. "I had a good time tonight."

"Me, too. Thanks for indulging me with my flower fascination."

"Are you planning on going to church on Sunday?" Billy asked.

"I go every Sunday with Gran."

"I just finished up a big job outside of Albany that's kept me away for six weeks, but I'll be there this Sunday."

There was a pause and Elise realized he was waiting for an invitation to sit next to her and Gran, but that was a pretty big step in their tight-knit community. It was like raising a banner up on town square announcing: Billy Redford and Elise Gibson are dating!

"I'll look for you. Are they having a potluck this week?" Elise knew that they weren't but it took the pressure off the seating arrangement.

Billy didn't seem to notice the deliberate change of subject. "I'm not sure, but I'd hate to miss it. I'm ready to put down roots in this place."

"You already have roots," Elise said. "This will always be your hometown."

"I like the sound of that." He stepped closer and pulled her into a hug. "I like you too, Elise."

She rested her head on his shoulder, liking the way her face was so close to his that she could feel his breath tickle her skin. Leaning back, Elise looked into his striking blue eyes. His gaze strayed to her lips and Elise felt her pulse quicken. Was he thinking of kissing her? She'd never admit how many times she'd imagined kissing Billy Redford in high school. It was surreal to be staring your dream in the face. After all these years, she wasn't sure if she was ready for this moment. She lowered her eyes and moved to step out of his embrace. "Thanks for a wonderful evening, Billy."

He grabbed hold of her hand and tugged her toward him. "See you Sunday?"

"Yes." It took all her strength to walk away from Billy

and the smoldering look he was giving her. Once inside her home, she leaned against the front door. "I'm in trouble," she whispered. Her date with Billy had been fun and they'd connected, save for the moment when he called her Laney. Billy had almost kissed her, and he definitely wanted to see her again. She had another date with Wes tomorrow and she was looking forward to it with hesitant hope. Maybe it was better if she talked to him before and told him that she wasn't just a tourist attraction. Her toes curled into the rug and she wondered why that sounded like such a formidable task.

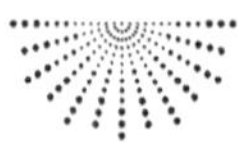

CHAPTER SEVENTEEN

The pavement was wet with an early morning rain storm when Elise drove to the B&B Saturday morning. She was walking toward the back entrance when she ran into Amy coming out, her camera bag slung over her shoulder.

"Hi Amy, what are you doing this morning?"

"I've been documenting your work in the theater room so Bonnie can get the web guy to put pictures up on the website." Amy patted her bag. "You're doing a great job."

"Thanks. I've snapped a few pictures with my phone, but I'd love to get some of yours for my portfolio."

"You bet. So how are things going with the prince?" Amy winked.

"Pretty good, he took me out on a date and it was

wonderful, but last night Billy Redford took me on a date and it was pretty wonderful too."

"Get out. Someone said Billy had moved back to town but I haven't seen him. Give me the deets."

"It was just a date, but we have so much in common," Elise said.

"Are you talking about the prince or Billy?"

"Both?" Elise grimaced. "I know it sounds terrible. I'm just confused about Wes's intentions."

"Have you gotten any pictures of him?" Amy asked.

"No, and I didn't ask him. He really hates the paparazzi."

"Man, do you have any idea how much one little picture of him in Echo Ridge could be worth?"

Elise folded her arms. "No, I haven't even considered it."

"One picture could pay all of your Grandma's taxes and repair your roof." Amy snapped her fingers. "Poof. Problems solved."

Elise looked down at the ground. Amy knew all about her problems—a month ago they'd spent a few days brainstorming ways to get the taxes paid, but this was not one of the ideas. "I care about Wes. I know it's just temporary, but I hope that we can be friends when he returns to Riodan."

"Oh, Elise. Guys aren't friends with girls. If he's

taking you out, spending time with you, it's because he likes you."

"Yes, but he lives on an island in the Caribbean so I think friends is sort of the only option since last I checked I'm a New Yorker."

"When is he going back home?"

"I don't know." Elise hoped that was a good sign that he was enjoying his time with her, but maybe he was trying to let her down easy. Her breath caught. He wouldn't leave without telling her, would he? An urgent feeling to see him washed over her. It was irrational, but Amy's chatter had faded into the background of her memory of Wes holding her hand, caressing her arm, touching her face. "I've got to run, okay. I'll catch up with you later."

Amy scowled. "Fine. I won't bring it up again. Tell me more about Billy."

"Oh, you mean about the roof?" Elise had laughter in her voice. "It was two-hundred dollars and he did great work. Gran and I are so relieved that the damage wasn't more extensive."

"So he does have it bad for you," Amy replied.

"What do you mean?"

"Two-hundred dollars would barely cover the materials he used to repair the roof. I wish I could find a nice guy like Billy." Amy looked past Elise's shoulder and she turned to see Billy's truck pulling into the B&B.

"Wait, he might have given me a little discount, but he didn't do the work for free," Elise said.

Amy raised her eyebrows. "I think you've been working at that flower shop too much because your head is full of pollen, but if you don't believe me, go ask him."

"Okay, maybe I will." Elise put her hands on her hips, watching Billy get out of his truck.

"That's my cue to leave," Amy said. "See you later."

Billy hoisted some kind of electric saw out of the back. When he looked up to see Elise watching him, he grinned and started toward her. "Good morning." He set the saw by the back door. "I'm just returning this to Carter. How are you doing?"

Elise tried to smile, but it felt crooked. "Billy, did you repair Gran's roof for free?"

He scrunched his eyebrows together. "I sent you the bill, didn't I?"

"No, I mean, for free labor."

Billy shrugged. "I sent you the bill."

Elise felt her face heat with the flush of humiliation. "Why did you tell me the roof only cost two-hundred dollars? I feel like I stole from you."

Billy hooked his thumbs in his belt loops. "I knew you wouldn't let me do it otherwise and it couldn't wait. Besides I had some extra shingles from another job.

They weren't a perfect match, but they were pretty close."

"But you shouldn't be doing stuff for free. It's not smart. This is your business."

"Exactly and I can run my business however I want. I know people think I'm just some dumb jock, but I actually have a few brain cells up here."

Elise gasped, stepping back as if he'd slapped her. "That's not true." But even as she said the words, she heard the tremor of her voice. She *had* remembered him as the star quarterback, the high school boy with muscles who didn't need straight A's to make it to college. Somehow Billy had caught the vibe that she'd unintentionally given. "I'm sorry," she mumbled.

"You don't have to do everything on your own. Pastor Louis told us last week that God is there willing to help us if we will let Him and that we are His hands. I was just trying to do something good."

Billy's words were like knives, cutting her feet out from under her and Elise remembered how desperately she'd kneeled and prayed for help. God had sent help and she was rejecting the miracle.

"I'm sorry," Elise repeated to Billy and the heavens. She squeezed her eyes tightly shut and heard the crunch of leaves on the sidewalk as Billy walked away. Elise felt a piece of her heart crumble under his steps. She hadn't decided how she felt about Billy romantically, but she never wanted to hurt him. "Wait, Billy, wait!" She hurried after him, grabbing his arm.

He stopped walking, but didn't look at her. "You're right." Elise said. "Exactly right about everything. I'm sorry." She let her hand fall from his arm and she looked down at the ground. "For most of my life it's just been me, my little brother, and Gran. There's never been a man to take care of me. I don't know what that's like and so I resist. I'm really confused about what I'm feeling right now. Please forgive me."

Billy blew out a breath. He took her hand, squeezing it gently and she lifted her eyes to his face. "Apology accepted. Try to remember that you don't hold the corner on the market for pain. Life is pain. Anyone who says differently is selling something."

Elise stepped back. Was Billy right? Did she hold everyone at arm's length because her father had abandoned her and she felt alone in the world surrounded by her pain for so long?

"I'll talk to you later, okay?"

Elise nodded. He let go of her hand and headed for his truck, not even glancing her way as he climbed inside. She still felt bad about the situation as he drove away, but she couldn't decide if it was the end of their dating relationship or not. She also couldn't decide if she wanted it to be or not. She really liked Wes, but she felt like she was stepping into an alternate reality every time she was with him. It was wonderful while they were together, but when she stepped back into her life, doubts swirled around her. Was she dreaming for the impossible?

CHAPTER EIGHTEEN

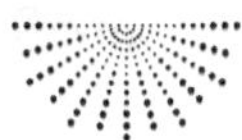

*E*lise's cell phone rang a few minutes later. She groaned when she saw Amy's face on her screen. Elise answered the phone. "You were right about Billy. He's a great guy and I really need to get some things done today."

"I hope you weren't too hard on him," Amy said. "Wait, I just saw him drive past me. What happened?"

Elise climbed the steps. "It's okay. We talked, but I don't want to talk about it right now. I'll catch up with you later."

"I'll be waiting," Amy grumbled, but even her grumble sounded good-natured.

Elise ended the call and stepped inside, letting her eyes adjust to the indoor lighting. She scanned the hallway and was grateful to find it empty. She'd been dreading this moment all morning, but Elise had to follow through with the right thing and that was to tell Wes about Billy. She climbed the steps to the third floor and went down another hallway to the master suite where Wes was staying. It was the best room at the Emerald Inn, "fit for a prince" according to Bonnie.

It was eight-fifteen so hopefully Wes was back from his run. She knocked lightly on the door, her stomach tying itself in knots. A moment later, the door swung open and Wes stood there shirtless with a plush white towel slung over his shoulder. He had shaving cream on one side of his face, but Elise wasn't looking at the black stubble on his chin. His chest was the perfect mix of lean and hard muscle, the precision of his pectorals to his abs was mouth-watering. Elise had never been the type to openly admire a man, but with Wes she couldn't help herself. Somehow she was able to engage her brain with her tongue. "Oh, gosh, I'm sorry. I didn't mean to bother you. I can wait."

"It's alright, why don't you come in. I'm almost done shaving." Wes stepped back, opening the door wider and motioning for her to come in.

And she thought she was in trouble last night. Someone upstairs must have a funny sense of humor when it came to testing her moral strength. "Are you sure? It's really not urgent, I just wanted to talk to you for a few minutes."

"I'm sure." Wes smiled at her as if he was quite aware

of the effect he was having on her. Elise rubbed the side of her mouth just in case she was drooling and followed Wes inside the suite. "This is a nice room. I haven't been up here for a long time."

"Oh, you've stayed here before?" Wes quirked an eyebrow.

She swatted his arm. "No, I've helped decorate a lot of these rooms. I created the theme for this room." She flourished an arm toward the royal blue and gold brocade bed skirt. "I sewed that and handstitched those tassels myself."

"I knew there was a reason I felt so at home in this room. You're very talented." Wes pointed at the photo of horses running through a mountain pasture. "I like the energy in that picture."

"Thanks. My friend, Amy took that photo. She lives here in Echo Ridge and is always toting her camera around taking pictures."

"It's nice, did she take the one of the sunrise over the lake too?" he inclined his head toward the photo hanging in the bathroom.

"Yes, that's Chickadee Lake."

"I thought so," Wes said. "This is a pretty area." He walked back to the sink where his razor waited on a white washcloth. His jeans hung just right across his hips and his bare feet poked out from the frayed hem. "Let me just finish up."

Elise stared at him in the mirror, hoping he would finish soon so that he could put on a shirt, or maybe that was what she should have been thinking. He finished shaving and washed his face off. The water shimmered down his dark skin and when he dried off, Wes caught her eye in the mirror and winked. Elise covered her eyes with one hand. "Do you have any idea what you're doing to me right now?"

"The same thing you're doing to me?" Wes sounded much closer than he'd been a second ago.

Elise dropped her hand and jumped. He stood in front of her, a big grin on his face.

"What did you need to talk to me about?" he leaned closer, his low voice rumbling.

"Um, I seem to have lost my train of thought. Maybe I should wait outside until you're ready."

Wes chuckled and reached behind her to grab his shirt off the bed. He pulled the dark gray and blue shirt over his head and Elise almost groaned out loud as his muscles flexed to pull the fabric down. She was losing her nerve, so she blurted out. "I wanted to talk to you before our date tonight. Last night I went out on a date with a guy I went to high school with. I hadn't seen him in forever and I didn't really know what to expect, but Billy wants to take me out again. I know we've only gone on one date, but, well, I was really looking forward to tonight and I'm not really sure what the protocol is in this situation."

Wes listened and nodded once. "Do you like this Billy?"

"He's a good guy and he lives here in Echo Ridge. I enjoyed spending time with him last night, but I enjoyed our date too. Does that make any sense?"

"Yes, thanks for telling me," Wes said. "While you're at it, why don't you give me a nice paper cut and pour lemon juice on it?"

"Oh dear. I didn't mean it that way. I just—I don't know what my problem is. What's the saying—painfully honest?" Elise clasped her hands together, waiting under the intensity of Wes's scrutiny. It was awkward, but she felt so much better letting him know what was going on in her dating life.

Wes sighed. "I think beautifully honest is how I would describe you."

Elise's head snapped up and a smile spread across her face. "Really?"

"I think you're the first woman I've ever dated who isn't afraid of honesty. I love it. I don't love that someone else wants to take you out on a date, but I hope you'll still go with me tonight because I have some great things planned."

"I'll be ready." She put her small hand on his large forearm. "Thanks for understanding."

Wes pulled her hand up to his face and kissed her palm. A thrill shot through her body and zinged out her toes. She curled her fingers in slowly and pulled her hand back to her heart. "I'll see you later."

"I can't wait," Wes said.

Elise glided down the stairs to the basement of the B&B. The movie posters didn't look as glamorous today because nothing could hold a candle to the real life romance she was in right now. Her date was still on with Wes tonight and there were some expectations on Sunday for Billy, so the pressure to make a good decision hovered over her. But talking to Wes had felt so right. It didn't solve her problem of what to do about Billy, but Elise gave herself permission to take a little time to figure out what her heart needed.

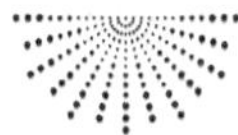

CHAPTER NINETEEN

Wes couldn't wipe the grin off his face after Elise left his suite. The way she'd openly admired him was a compliment, but the thing that made his blood pump was her brutal honesty. She wasn't afraid to talk to him about something that most people would have kept secret. It made him that much happier that he had decided to pay her taxes. That secret warmed in his chest and made him smile wider. His cell phone rang and Wes didn't cringe like he usually did when he saw his mother's picture on his screen.

"Hello Mother, I hope you're doing well."

"I am, but I don't think I'm doing as well as you are. You sound quite different from our last conversation."

"I'm happy. It's beautiful here in New York and I've had time to figure some things out for my project. I think it's going to be a success and really change some lives."

"Good, it sounds like you could come home this weekend then, right?"

"Why?"

His mother tsked. "People are starting to talk. They worry about our family and the stability of the crown. You may not have realized the calming influence you have on all of us. We miss you."

"Thanks, Mother, but I'm not ready to come home yet. Maybe once things are sorted out with Titan."

"Darling, that could be years. Your brother is in a lot of trouble and we're working to get him into a specialized rehabilitation center on another island."

"Will he go?"

"I think to stay out of jail he might."

Wes's heart hurt when he thought of the pain his older brother had caused his family. "I'm sorry, Mother."

"Weston, what's really keeping you there? Why won't you come home?"

"I told you. I've been busy and I haven't had to worry about distractions so I've accomplished a lot."

"Have you met someone?" There was a strange tone to his mother's voice, partial hope mixed with fear.

He groaned. She knew. Those guards of hers must be reporting every detail to his parents. Still, there was no way he was going to answer that question, but before he could say anything his mom cleared her throat. "I'm not sure what you feel for this young woman, but you should know that she's dating someone else."

"So you're watching me and Elise?" It took all his strength to keep his voice even.

"Standard protocol. Weston, I don't want to be hurtful, but you're probably just a fling for her. I'm surprised that we haven't seen pictures on the tabloids yet."

"Mother, she's not like that. And I already knew that she went on a date with someone else. That's what people do when they are dating. They date people."

The queen sniffed. "I'm glad to know that you still have your head about you, but I've never seen you date someone like her before."

Wes could hear the disdain in his mother's voice and he wished that she could know Elise the way that he did. "You don't know anything about her."

"Oh, on the contrary. We know everything about her."

"Fine, then you know that she is a charming and devoted granddaughter and respected citizen of Echo Ridge."

"Be careful dear," his mother replied. "You're not like Titan. You have a gentle heart. And Wes, please do your homework. I sent you the royal decree from the original Montoya ruling days ago. You need to study it."

"Okay, I'll do it."

After Wes hung up, he closed his eyes, replaying the conversation in his mind. Of course his mother didn't approve of Elise, but there was something to smile about. In her search to dig up dirt on the Gibson's, she had found none or else she would have reported it. That was something that rarely happened. Wes opened his eyes and nodded. Maybe he could prove his mother wrong for once. He swiped the screen on his phone and searched through his email until he found the note from his mother with a lengthy document attached. Trying to read it on his phone would give him a headache, he'd have to look at it on his laptop. Before he had a chance to login to his computer, his phone rang with one of his business associates. The royal decree would have to wait.

Wes had told Elise to dress nice, but casual. So she tugged on boot-cut jeans with her favorite square-toed cowboy boots. She wore a long-sleeved fitted white blouse with splashes of color in yellow and orange. Elise analyzed her feelings concerning the two men vying for her attention. Last night had been fun with Billy, but tonight she could hardly keep the smile from her face every time she thought of Wes. What did that mean? She didn't want to be a fling with Wes and she didn't feel that way, but he was still a Riodanian prince. Elise closed her eyes and offered up a prayer that the Lord would give her the direction she needed to make the right decision when the time came.

"Your gorgeous prince is here again," Gran called up the stairs.

Elise's eyes widened. Had Gran figured out the secret too? She scrambled down the stairs, hoping that Wes hadn't made it through the door, but he was there waiting with Gran. "I didn't tell her." She looked at Wes with a pleading expression, and then turned to Suzy, "Gran, how did you know?"

Gran made a clicking noise with her tongue. "I don't know why you thought I wouldn't notice when the best-looking prince from Riodan came to my home. I may be old, but I can still see just fine with my glasses."

Wes burst out laughing, probably at the flabbergasted expression on Elise's face. He stepped forward and took her hand. "I think she's speechless because she didn't know who I was when we first met."

"Is that so?" Gran stood up straighter. "Well, finally I'm more current than my granddaughter, but don't you worry, your highness. I haven't told a soul."

"It's Wes, and thank you." He turned to Elise. "You look lovely. Are you ready?"

"Yes, let's go before Gran embarrasses me further."

"You two have fun," Gran said. "I'll be in bed."

"Good night, Gran." Elise gripped Wes's hand and pulled him forward.

"Love you dear," Gran called after her.

"I love you too."

"Good night," Wes called as the screen door slammed shut behind him. Wes put his hand on the small of her back and guided her to his rental car. "Your Gran makes me miss my sisters. They love to tease me like crazy and I hold my own."

"I bet you do," Elise said. She let him help her into the car and she sank back into the leather seats. Wes started the car and flicked on the heat. Spring had arrived in Echo Ridge, but the temperature dropped quickly at night. "So where are we going?"

"Not telling," Wes said. "I like surprises."

Wes reached across the car and tickled her side until she squealed. He continued driving through town and then he turned toward the B&B. "Wait a minute, are we going to the B&B? Did you forget something?"

Wes didn't say anything. He just smiled, pulled into the parking lot and hopped out of the car. He opened her door. "I didn't forget anything. I have you, don't I?" He held out his hand and helped her from the car.

His words jolted through her and Elise clasped his hand tightly, wishing she had the nerve to ask what he meant exactly. "So we are going here? Should I be worried?"

Wes chuckled. "We aren't going to my suite. I reserved the private dining room. I hope you don't mind. I was going to take you to the seafood fest at the tulip festival, but with all the people and press, I couldn't talk myself into it."

Elise tucked her arm in his. "I think that sounds perfect."

Even though she'd spent every day over the past couple weeks at the B&B, she'd never ventured into the dining room. Wes led her inside and slid the outer door shut behind them. Low lights in the corners illuminated a table set for two with candles flickering gently. The resident chef appeared after Wes helped Elise sit down. Amos had fluffy white hair and a thick mustache to match. His face was lined with laughter and his talent in the kitchen was well known in Echo Ridge. He entered the dining room with the air of a gentleman about him, a white cloth over his arm and a basket of crusty Italian bread in the other hand. Elise's mouth watered. Amos put two dipping bowls with garlic infused olive oil and balsamic vinegar on the table.

"I'll be back with your salads in a moment." He winked at Elise and she nodded.

Their chairs were set next to each other, with Wes at the head of the table and Elise seated at his right. It felt intimate and comfortable. Elise put her hand on his arm. "This is so romantic. Thank you."

"I'm glad you like it. I was worried you might be sick of this place." Wes ripped his bread in half and immersed it in the oil. He took a bite, closing his eyes. "Mmm, this is delicious."

"I look forward to coming here every day," Elise said. She took a bite of bread, savoring the chewy crust and soft, flaky inside. "The theater remodel has been one of my favorite projects and I have you to thank for that."

Amos brought out their salads and a house vinaigrette that smelled like lemon and basil. Wes was quiet for a moment as they ate their salads, but Elise could feel a conversation brewing under the surface and wondered what was on his mind. For once she didn't speak; she smiled and ate her salad. Finally, Wes put down his fork and Elise looked at him expectantly.

"My mother keeps asking when I'm going to come home."

So this was it. He had planned this intimate dinner so that he could tell her goodbye. Elise steeled herself for the words that would come next. She clutched her fork so tight, the metal bit into her skin.

"I told her that I didn't want to come home yet, because I love it here," Wes said.

Elise's fork clattered against her plate. Of course, that was the moment Amos decided to bring out the honey glazed salmon.

"Here you are my dear," he placed the plate gently in

front of her, oblivious of her thoughts like firecrackers shooting in every direction. Wes wasn't going home. He wasn't telling her goodbye, but what was he telling her? As soon as Amos returned to the kitchen, Elise found her voice.

"So are you staying here because you like Echo Ridge so much?

Wes took her hand in his. "I'm saying that my work isn't finished here and I'm not ready to go home. Elise, I've never met anyone like you before. I can't stop thinking about you. When I told my mother I wasn't coming home, she asked me if I'd met someone."

Elise swallowed as she thought of what the queen of Riodan would say about her son dating an American. "What did you say?"

"I didn't answer, of course, but she knew because she told me to be careful with my heart." Wes lowered his voice as he leaned toward Elise. "But she warned me too late."

Warmth flooded from Elise's heart through her fingertips that were wrapped tightly around Wes's hand. "I don't know what to say."

"Well, that would definitely be a first." Wes smiled.

Elise stuck out her tongue. "I'm surprised because I've been trying to prepare myself for the time when you'd have to leave. I didn't like the thought but I've held myself back because I'm worried about one word in everything you've told me."

Wes furrowed his brow in question.

"Yet," Elise said. "You're not ready to go home *yet*, but eventually you will go home."

Wes nodded. "You're right. I do have to go home. I'm not an American citizen so I can't stay here indefinitely, but until then I'd like to date you."

The prince of Riodan had just told Elise that he wanted to date her—the unknown woman from Echo Ridge. This was what she'd been hoping and praying for. Wes was letting her know very clearly that he wasn't messing around, he was interested in the future with her. She pressed her lips together, staring into Wes's eyes as he searched her face for acceptance of his request. "I'd love to have more time with you, but I'm not very good at goodbyes, so then what?"

"How about we take it one day at a time for now?"

Elise nodded. "I can do that." But could she really? Her heart might break.

Wes picked up her fork carefully and placed it in her fingers. "Let's eat this salmon before it goes cold."

The food was delicious, but the best part of the meal was the way Wes kept looking at Elise with promise and adoration in his eyes. Or maybe that was just her wishful thinking, but she felt light with energy sparkling through every look they shared. Wes asked her questions about her childhood and she told him about the good parts she remembered before her mom died. After a rough period of adjustment, her later teen years in her Gran's house were a blessing, and her brother Mark had a special place in her heart as well. To grow up surrounded by music and love despite losing both her parents was truly a blessing. "There were definitely times when I wished for parents like my friends had, but Grandma Suzy gave me a different perspective on life that I don't think I could've gained anywhere else."

"When I was a kid, I saw a movie about the prince and the pauper and I used to wish that I could run away and switch places with someone so I wouldn't have to study with my private tutors." Wes dabbed his mouth with his napkin. "It took me working on a service project in the underprivileged section of Riodan to understand exactly what I had taken for granted. My education could've changed some of those people's lives and helped them escape the slums. My studies were different after that. At least until I turned sixteen and noticed girls."

Elise smiled. "I'm sure they noticed you long before that."

"I was a gangly kid with hair that stood straight up." Wes ran his hand over his hair. "I keep it much shorter now."

"Did you ever try to escape the palace?"

"Once, and that's when I found out how many undercover guards my father employed. He wasn't very happy."

"Do you get along with your father?" Elise finished her last bite of salmon.

Wes leaned back and folded his hands over his stomach. "We have a different relationship. He's always been busy, absorbed, even when he was with the family. I can't pretend to understand all the pressure he's constantly under but I do know that he's a good man and he tries to do what's right."

"I'm glad to hear that."

"I wish I could say the same about Titan," Wes shook his head.

Elise brushed her fingers over his. "I'm sorry about the turmoil he's caused your family."

"I hope that we've come up with a solution. If my parents decide to go for it, Titan will have his whole world turned on its end and he'll be forced to choose a different way of life than his playboy lifestyle."

"That sounds pretty incredible, but how can anyone manage that?" Elise asked.

"I've been talking with my mother and I gave her the idea to force Titan to live among the disadvantaged in Riodan and find a way to rise up nobly in order to return to the palace."

"They would do that?"

Wes pursed his lips together and blew a breath through his nose. "It's either forced community service or jail time for Titan. I'm pretty sure they're going to try something. Of course, I'm not even supposed to know this, but mother sounded different when I talked to her last—like something big is coming."

Elise nodded. Amos arrived to clear their plates before she could say more, but the implications of what Wes had revealed spun through her mind. That kind of treatment would shine the light even brighter on the Montoya family. No wonder Wes wanted to stay in Echo Ridge longer. Amos served them chocolate mousse dotted with raspberries in chilled china bowls.

"Thank you, Amos," Wes said. "This has been excellent."

"Yes, and this looks delicious," Elise added. "I'm going to have to get your recipe for that salmon. It was so light and flaky."

Amos beamed with pride. "You come to the kitchen and I'll teach you myself."

Elise nodded. "I just might do that."

Amos bowed and excused himself to the kitchen.

"Do you know what I love most about this evening?" Wes asked.

She held her spoon up with a heaping spoonful of fluffy chocolate. "The mousse?"

He smiled. "That and the fact that I haven't had to

worry about anyone recognizing me or asking to take pictures with me. I know it won't last forever, but I enjoy my privacy and especially having you here to share this time with me."

"I'm sorry that you have to deal with that all the time," Elise said. "It must be hard to find some kind of normal."

Wes nodded. They finished their meal and Wes stood, stretching towards the ceiling. He was so tall and broad that when Elise stood next to him, she felt dainty. Wes put his hand on the small of her back and guided her through the entrance of the B&B. "I have one more thing planned, if you don't mind."

Elise glanced at her watch. "It's only seven-thirty. The night's young. I have several hours before I turn into a pumpkin."

Wes chuckled. "In that case, I may have a few more things planned." He lifted his eyebrows and Elise felt her cheeks redden. She gripped his hand as they walked out to his car. Once they were buckled in, he headed up toward Ruby Mountain, the car shifting into gear to climb the steep mountain. Wes pulled up to Parley's lookout.

Everyone knew about the Echo Ridge lookout, it was a regular patrol area for the police, but it also had the best view of the stars. Elise had only come to the lookout a couple times as a teenager and that was with a big group of friends. She'd secretly imagined going with Billy Redford, but that dream seemed all wrong now.

"How did you know about this place?" Elise asked after Wes helped her out of the car.

"I have good sources." He spread a blanket on the hood and lifted Elise onto the car, carefully climbing up next to her.

"Sources? Like your security guards, or what?"

"Bonnie is pretty helpful." Wes put his arm around Elise and murmured, "And you should know that she wants to be invited to our wedding."

"What?" Elise gasped and Wes laughed. She laughed along with him, covering her mouth. "Bonnie is the one who told me about you."

"Really?"

"She spotted your security detail."

Wes chuckled. "I'll have to tell my mother that story. Bonnie must not have told anyone else, though." He gestured to the sky. "The stars were bright on the way up here, but the clouds are coming back in."

"Yeah, I don't think people do much star gazing in April."

They leaned back against the windshield and pointed out a few constellations. Elise shivered as the night cooled and the clouds covered the remaining stars. Then she felt a drop of rain on her cheek. Wes gently wiped away the moisture with his thumb.

"So what do people do at eight-thirty on a Saturday night in Echo Ridge when it's raining?" he asked.

"Go home and eat ice cream?" Elise offered.

"Really? That sounds perfect." He jumped down from the car and put his arms around Elise, lifting her to the ground. She would have loved to stand there, but she felt another drop of rain hit the top of her head. Wes helped her into the car and tossed the blanket in the back seat. He jogged around to his side and started the car. "Should we stop by the store and grab some or does your Grandma keep the freezer stocked?"

Elise smiled. "Gran always has at list six different kinds of ice cream so we're prepared."

"Prepared for what?"

"Everything." Elise held up her hand and let it drop.

He steered onto the mountain road. They coasted down quickly and ten minutes later were heading through town. Wes tapped the steering wheel. "Okay, what's your flavor?"

"Chocolate peanut butter. You?"

"Vanilla."

Elise wrinkled her nose. "You're not serious. You are so not a vanilla flavored guy."

That elicited a deep chuckle from Wes. "You got me. I like mint fudge."

"That is nuts. That's Gran's favorite."

"It's a sign then."

"For what?"

Wes pulled into her driveway. "That we should eat two bowls instead of one."

The rain was still a light sprinkle, but the sky was heavy with clouds that promised more precipitation. Elise liked the way Wes took her hand and guided her up the stairs to her house. They dished up the ice cream and Elise pulled out the toppings. Wes snagged the hot fudge and scooped out a large dollop. Elise arched an eyebrow. "Planning on becoming a diabetic?"

Wes chuckled. "Never go up against a Riodanian when chocolate is on the line."

Elise laughed, snorted, and covered her mouth. She couldn't believe she'd just snorted in front of a prince, but he didn't seem to mind. He licked the thick chocolate fudge off the spoon and smiled. "Our country exports cacao beans. It's one of my favorite commodities."

"Your country sounds delicious." They swirled caramel, chopped nuts, and a large squirt of whipped cream over their bowls of coma-inducing sugar. "I'm sorry that we're out of cherries," Elise said.

"I think I'll manage." Wes twirled his spoon in and out of his fingers.

Elise led Wes into their family room where they sat next to each other on the sofa. "Gran must be in bed already or I'm sure she would have come down when she heard the chink of the ice cream scoop."

Wes put a large spoonful of the minty green ice cream in his mouth. "Mmm. Tell your Gran thanks for sharing her ice cream."

Even watching him eat ice cream increased her heart rate. Elise scooped up a spoonful of chocolate ice cream rippled with peanut butter. She flipped the spoon over in her mouth and slowly pulled it out.

"My sister does that," Wes said, watching her.

"It's the only way to eat ice cream." Elise took another bite and smiled at Wes. He stared at her, a look of appreciation in his eyes. "What?" she asked.

He looked down at his ice cream and his lips twitched. "You fascinate me—the way you relish life. You live so strong and grab your joy. I want to know how you do that."

Elise took the spoon from his hand and scooped up the mint ice cream. She held it up to his mouth and he raised his eyebrows. "Like this," she said. She pushed the spoon forward until he opened his mouth, and at the last second she flipped it over. He swallowed his ice cream and they both started laughing. Wes set their bowls on the coffee table in front of them and pulled her close into his chest. He kissed her forehead and Elise held perfectly still as the moment cascaded over her. She was in the arms of a prince and she was going to ignore the reality-check devil that told her this couldn't last. Elise snuggled into him and sighed.

"Elise?" his voice was just above a whisper.

"Yeah?"

"I hope you don't mind my asking, but, am I getting in the way of a potential relationship with that other guy?"

"Billy?" Elise sat up. "No, I mean yes, from his viewpoint, but…" She furrowed her brow, trying to think of the right words.

"So he wants more than you do?" Wes's voice held a note of hopefulness.

Elise nodded. "I'll be honest. I've had a hard time knowing what to do because I had a crush on Billy in high school. It was my dream to go out on a date with him. But tonight when I was getting ready to go out with you, I was so excited my heart was doing back flips. I realized that's how it should be. I prayed that the Lord would help me make the right decision because I wanted to have a chance with you."

Wes grinned. "So, did you get your answer?"

"Yes. I'm not interested in dating Billy. He's a great guy and a good friend, but I don't have the same feelings for him that I do for you."

Wes pulled her against his chest again and she melted into his embrace. "I love your honesty."

Elise hugged him, loving the feel of his heart beating

against her cheek. She felt so comfortable that she almost responded with an I love you before catching herself and saying, "Thank you."

"Elise?" Wes's voice was husky and low.

She smiled. "Yeah?"

"Thanks for sharing your joy with me."

Elise sat up and put her hand on his cheek. She wasn't from Riodan, but Wes was here in front of her right now and all the reasons that they couldn't be together didn't seem to matter as he pulled her closer. His lips covered hers in a gentle kiss that turned hungry. She grabbed his shirt and felt his hands move down her back, tightening around her waist. A soft moan escaped her and Wes moved his lips along the curve of her jaw and down her neck. She leaned her head back, feeling the heat of his kisses searing into her skin. Her arms encircled his neck and she pulled his mouth back up to hers, kissing him with a passion she didn't know was possible. Every nerve ending sparkled with energy and Elise felt more alive than she'd ever been. Wes held her fiercely, yet gently at the same time, as if he'd never let her go. She was lost in his embrace, in his kiss where no oceans stood between them.

Elise pulled back, but Wes held her tight, kissing around her upper lip. She put her hand on his cheek and leaned her forehead against his, their breaths moving in tandem.

"I guess it's time for me to go home," he murmured, his breath hot against her cheek.

"Mmm, hmm." She tilted her head to rest on his shoulder, and let her hand trail down his chest, his sculpted chest easily defined under his thin t-shirt.

Wes scooped her up as he stood and held her close to him. She could see the desire in his eyes and she was certain he was getting the same vibe from her. He carefully released her to a standing position where she stood, still clinging to him. There were so many words she wanted to say, to ask him what this kiss meant. What all of his time and attention meant when he lived in a different world, one she doubted she could ever be a part of. When she opened her mouth, Wes leaned forward and kissed the words away. She forgot her questions and focused on how he lifted her feet off the ground with his tight embrace. Somehow they made it to the front porch, still kissing and communicating something much stronger than words.

Elise felt like she was standing on a tropical beach, with the hot sand warming the soles of her feet. "I wish you didn't have to go," Elise murmured, and she meant more than just that night. She didn't want Wes to ever leave her. If he asked her, she was pretty sure that she'd follow him across the seas right that moment, until she remembered Gran. That thought pulled her back to the present and she reached her toes toward the ground until she was standing on her own two feet again.

Wes kissed her once more. "I don't want to leave either, but I'd better let you get some sleep. And I'll have to stop kissing you in order to do that."

Elise smiled and walked him to the front door. "Thanks again for tonight."

"My pleasure," she murmured. They stood on the porch staring out at the darkened sky, neither wanting the night to end.

"I'll see you tomorrow then?" Elise touched his cheek, letting her fingers trail down his neck and brush against the coarse hair at the nape of his neck.

"Tomorrow." He stepped down, but Elise grabbed his hand pulling him toward her. She didn't want the magic of the night to end. Wes closed the distance and kissed her softly, pressing his hands against her back as she put her arms around his neck. His lips caressed hers until they both were breathless. Elise's heart thrummed happily in her chest as he leaned back, touched her cheek with his fingertips and whispered, "Good night."

Wes turned and jogged down the steps to his car. As he got inside, Elise thought she saw a flicker of light and she looked toward the sky. It was dotted with stars heavy in between the clouds that threatened more rain.

"Good night," she called.

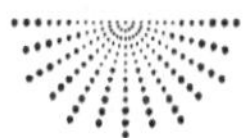

CHAPTER TWENTY

Wes wanted to come to church with Elise, but she told him it wasn't worth blowing his cover. One of the parishioners would definitely recognize him. He looked more like Titan than he probably wanted to with his sculpted cheekbones and sculpted body. Elise thought briefly about skipping church to have brunch with Wes, but now was probably the best time to face Billy. After the kiss to end all kisses last night, Weston had ruined any chance she might have had of a relationship with Billy. It was difficult to follow her heart and ignore her head, but she had to be honest with herself and Billy.

The church was packed and Gran found their usual pew near the front next to some of her friends. Elise squeezed in next to Gran, grateful that the bench was full and she wouldn't have to face the awkward moment of sitting next to Billy during services. But then Milo and Britta saw someone come in the back. They waved and moved to sit next to Anika, Carlos, and their darling daughter Megan. Elise smiled at the two love stories she'd witnessed in Echo Ridge in the last year. She turned to face the front at the same moment Billy sat down next to her.

"Good morning," he said in a low voice. "Thanks for saving me a seat."

"I didn't—uh, know if you were going to make it," Elise said, scrambling for a response because she hadn't been saving him a seat.

Billy smiled. "I couldn't miss it."

Pastor Louis talked about honesty with our fellow man and God. He expounded on how living an honest life was the only path to true happiness. Elise felt guilty listening to the sermon and sitting next to Billy where the entire congregation would see and take note. She didn't want to hurt Billy, but she needed to talk to him. As soon as the sermon was over, she took his hand. "Do you have a minute to talk?"

"Sure." His face was open and eager. Elise might as well have been pulling a cannon behind her to shoot Cupid out of the sky as they exited the church and walked to a shade tree in the back. The tree had bright green leaves, shooting out in every direction, glossy under the morning sunlight. Elise focused on the rebirth of spring all around them, hoping that she could find the right words for Billy.

He took her hand and pulled her into a hug. "I've missed you."

Elise forced a smile and carefully moved out of his embrace. "That was a great sermon. It got me thinking about my life and everything that's happened lately."

"Me, too. I couldn't stop thinking about you…and me." Billy stepped forward and grazed her cheek with his fingertips, cupping her chin. "Elise, you're good for me. Not many people want to live in Echo Ridge, they don't understand what it's like here."

A niggling doubt lingered that whispered for her to keep her mouth shut. When Wes returned to Riodan without her, Elise would still be in Echo Ridge and Billy was a great guy. Once she let Billy go, she'd never get another chance. She covered his fingertips with hers and pulled his hand from her cheek. "Billy, this is so hard for me, but I can't do this right now."

"What do you mean?"

"I need to be fair to you and me. You're a great guy, but I don't think I'm the girl you're looking for. I'm not Laney and I never will be."

"I told you that didn't mean anything," Billy said.

"I know, but it made me realize that maybe we just wanted to spend time with each other because it felt familiar to us. Maybe you don't really like me, but you like the idea of me. I'm someone safe and I feel the same way about you, but for some reason I need to take a big risk with my heart. If I don't do it now, I'm not sure I'll ever get another chance."

He opened his mouth and Elise touched his lips with her finger. "Shh, I know I do most of the talking anyway, but I need to say this."

He nodded, the hurt already edging the outer rim of his blue eyes.

"I can't date you right now," Elise said. "When we went on that first date, I didn't expect things to move along so quickly. I can see now that you're ready for a serious relationship and I need more time to figure out my life." The words were on the tip of her tongue. She wanted to tell him that she was dating Wes, but how could she do that without revealing the secret she'd promised to keep? That truth would also inflict unnecessary pain on Billy if her relationship couldn't cross the borders of the ocean with Wes. Billy had already lost Laney to another man, it wasn't fair to crush him. She touched his cheek and then lowered her hand. Billy grabbed onto it.

"Let's take a break. I didn't mean to come on so strong," he said, desperation creeping into his voice. "I can give you time."

The breath caught in her throat and she swallowed. "I think we should both date other people for a while."

Billy nodded. "Okay, that's a good idea, but can I still see you? Maybe in a few weeks?"

Elise didn't want to give him false hope. Wes had her heart and if things didn't work out for them, she'd be in no state to pursue another relationship. The thought of losing Wes caused a streak of pain to radiate through her chest. "Billy, I can't thank you enough for what you've done for me. I'm sorry I wasn't as appreciative of the work you did on our roof—you know, because of the deal you gave us."

He waved his hand. "That's okay. I understand."

"But more than that," Elise said. "I'm glad that I got to know you because you showed me how good someone can be. And that we all have a chance to grow up, change, and be better. I'm still working on that, but thank you for your example."

"I could say the same about you." He squeezed her hand. "Don't forget me okay?"

"I won't. Take care of your heart. It's a good one." Elise looked him in the eyes one last time and then turned, walking away quickly before her good sense convinced her not to go chasing after fairy tales. Her throat hurt from tightening it to keep the emotions at bay and when she glanced back she saw Billy walking to his truck, his shoulders slumped. Her eyes burned with tears and she offered up a silent prayer that God would watch over Billy and send him the right woman. She added onto that prayer that somehow she could find a way to be with Wes, because thinking of the alternative was too painful to bear.

Elise walked around the church and took a few minutes to compose herself. She was headed to her car when she ran into Amy.

"Did you hear about Prince Titan?" Amy was almost breathless.

"No, what happened?"

"He is no longer the crown prince." Amy put her hand on Elise's arm. "He was ejected from the palace and stripped of his title. He has to live among the commoners until he proves himself worthy of the royal family. The Montoyas made an official statement. It's all over every news page."

"What? Are you sure it's legit?" Elise couldn't let on that she knew any of the details Wes had shared with her about the Montoyas, but she was still surprised that the royals had went ahead with Weston's suggestion, and apparently taken things a step further.

"Look at this article." Amy shoved her phone under Elise's nose where the headline news streamed across the small screen. Elise squinted and shifted the phone so that she could read the article:

Breaking news. Crown prince Titan Montoya was ordered by royal decree to live in the public sector among the poorest citizens of Riodan. He will maintain an armed guard, but his title was stripped. With only sixty-five Riodanian rounds, roughly equivalent to one-hundred-thirty US dollars, he was charged to make a living for himself honestly before he could return to the palace.

The official statement did not extrapolate on this punishment, but speculations about Titan's behavior and the effect it has had on the Montoya family name are certainly to blame. Officials of Riodan cite an ancient decree that can shift the heir of the crown to any son in the royal family. Citizens have already picked their favorite, but we're waiting for notice from King Bastian before we give further speculation.

Elise handed the phone back to Amy. "I guess I need to pay better attention to the news."

"Um, yeah, because guess who the next contender for the crown is?" Amy leaned forward on her tiptoes.

"Zac? I can't remember all of their names." Elise shrugged.

"Really? Sometimes I think you ignore stuff on purpose," Amy said. "Your prince Weston has been named as the successor."

"But that article just said they are still waiting for the royal announcement," Elise replied.

Amy waved her phone back and forth. "But everyone already knows it will be Weston. He's the most accomplished, level-headed son. And you're dating him!"

"Shh, now it will be even more important for Wes to keep a low profile." Elise frowned. Would this news drive Wes from Echo Ridge forever? "I'd better go. I hope no one finds out he's here."

"I think it's a little late for that now. Someone will recognize him, probably several have wondered already," Amy said. "It's only a matter of time."

Elise hesitated, narrowing her eyes. "Don't sound so happy about that, okay?"

"Sorry, it's kind of cool that Echo Ridge could be the center of the biggest news story of the year."

It was then that Elise noticed the camera bag Amy always had with her. It looked like a chic purse, but it held an expensive and sophisticated camera. Amy looked almost hungry as she talked about the potential for news. The realization pierced her heart. Even though it was the last thing Elise wanted, it was time for Wes to leave. "I'll see you later." She waved at Amy and jogged to her car.

There was a news van in front of the B&B when Elise arrived. Her stomach sank as she recognized a reporter for NY5 News behind the wheel of a black SUV. They couldn't enter the B&B, but if they saw her, it might make things worse. She drove past the B&B, parked on a side street and pulled a jacket out of her trunk. She pulled on the hood, tucking her dark hair in and blessed the idea she'd had that morning to wear flats and a comfortable skirt. Heavy clouds moved over the sun as she approached the B&B from the back and slipped in through the service entrance.

She didn't speak to anyone when she entered through the kitchen of the B&B. It was bustling with mid-morning baking and Amos was hunting through his spice cabinet so she entered the main hallway and dashed up the stairs as fast as she could to the master suite. Knocking softly, Elise prayed that Wes was there. Briefly, she wondered if he'd already heard about the news and had left town, but a few seconds later, the door swung open.

"Wes, you're here. Thank goodness. Did the reporters see you yet?" Elise flipped her hood back and moved to step forward, but Wes folded his arms, his stance similar to a brick wall. He glared at Elise and she felt the venom in his stare so powerfully that she took a step back. "Wes?"

He unfolded his arms and Elise saw that he held a newspaper. He shoved it in her direction and she opened her hands to catch it. The paper unfolded to reveal a front page spread with a bold headline: **Riodan's New Crown Prince Kissing an American Commoner**

The air felt like it was pulled from her lungs as Elise tried to focus on the picture. It was her and Wes standing on her Grandma's front porch, arms around each other in an intimate kiss.

"How could you let this happen?" Wes hissed.

Elise's head snapped up. "Me? I didn't have anything to do with this. I'm *in* the picture with you." That had been one of the happiest moments of her life, filled with promise, love, and fireworks. How could Wes think that she would exploit him? She smoothed out the paper in her hand and scanned the article. It only took two seconds for her to find the photo credit to A+ Photography. "Amy," she breathed. "She didn't." But she did. The evidence was in her hands, available for millions of people to see.

"Did you really think you could get away with this? That I wouldn't discover the leak?"

"Wes, I didn't have anything to do with this. Amy must have followed us and taken the pictures." Elise held out the paper. "You remember this moment. It was between you and me, no one else. I'd never do that to you." Elise took a hesitant step forward and touched Wes's arm. "Please, can we talk about this?"

"I thought Amy was your friend," Wes said.

"I thought the same thing," Elise said. "I never thought she'd stoop this low. She said she needed money, but—"

"You need money too, to pay your taxes," Wes said quietly.

The words were just above a whisper but Elise felt like she'd been slapped. "Do you think so little of me?"

"I don't know what to think. You are the only one who knows me and you know about Titan too," he said.

"Plenty of people in this town knew you were here," Elise said. "If Bonnie recognized you, someone else did too."

"But how did Amy know? And how did she know where we would be to take that picture?"

Elise's heart stuttered. She looked up to Wes and noticed the hardness in his eyes. This was it. He was looking for someone to blame and he was going to blame her no matter what she said. Her eyes filled with tears. "I told her, but it was before I had talked to you—before you'd officially introduced yourself. I had no idea that she would betray me—you, like that. I'm sorry."

Wes stepped back and put his hand on the door. "I'm flying out in an hour." He started closing the door and Elise stepped forward and put her foot next to it.

"You're angry. I am too, but please, can't you see that I didn't do this? I would never hurt you."

"But you did." He pressed his lips together. "That picture is at your house and we weren't on the porch that long. You expect me to believe that Amy followed us and waited for hours to snap the picture?"

"Wes, I didn't do this," Elise protested, but Wes wasn't listening to her.

"You're not the first person to use me this way and that article is a complete lie. It says that I'm the new crown prince. That my brother deferred the crown." Wes pointed at the paper. "You knew about the plan to move Titan to the poor sector. It's part of an intervention that our whole family is doing. It was supposed to be a secret."

"I didn't tell anyone!" Elise cried. "But there was something in the article I read that I'd never heard before. Something about ancient protocol in Riodan. Does it sound familiar?"

"My family is strong and powerful. We aren't swayed by the world's views. My brothers are my blood. We are men of action, lies do not become us. Goodbye Elise." Wes closed the door.

When the latch clicked, Elise felt like her heart ripped in half. She put her hand over her mouth to cover the sob that punched the back of her throat with a force that made her shudder. Stumbling down the stairs, Elise ran to the back of the B&B. When she opened the door, she heard cameras clicking and flashing and several people yelled her name.

"Elise, can you tell us the state of your relationship with Prince Weston?"

"How long have you been dating the prince?"

"Is it true that you hired your friend to take pictures of you kissing the prince?"

Elise gasped, ducked her head, and ran as fast as she could away from the screaming reporters. She almost ran into the side of her car, the momentum, agony, and tears pushing at her with a horrible power that threatened to destroy her.

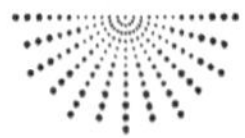

Wes wanted to punch the wall, but he decided to punch a pillow instead. That didn't help, so he slumped onto the floor, leaning against the bed, lowering his head onto his knees. He squeezed his eyes tight against the flashes of red anger that coursed through his veins every time he thought of the photo of him and Elise kissing. The moment, forever tainted, would be viewed by hundreds of millions of people by the week's end. The part that hurt the most was that Elise had betrayed him. He had trusted her implicitly, shared his family secrets, and she had kept his secrets from everyone but the one person who could destroy everything. Amy McCallister of A+ Photography was the one he should direct his blame and anger toward, but if Elise hadn't tipped her off, she never would've followed them and captured that shot.

The cherubic cupid on his shoulder whispered that he was wrong and unfair. Amy might have discovered his identity, just the same way that others in Echo Ridge had. He remembered seeing the tall, blond librarian heading into the building one morning. She'd done a double take when he ran past and he was almost sure she'd recognized him, but she only waved the next time he'd seen her.When he told Elise about that incident, she agreed that Britta would have kept his secret because she was that kind of person and friend. What he couldn't figure out was how Elise could call Amy a friend when she was capable of doing what she did.

And what did Elise mean when she said that Titan had been stripped of his crown? Wes hated the tabloids, but his curiosity finally got the better of him. He pulled up a couple articles on his phone before he found the information Elise had been referring to. It was all there —the official statement from the royals stating that Titan was no longer the crown prince. This was beyond what he'd asked his mother to consider. It seemed harsh and excessive and also unprecedented for a first-born son to lose his ranking.

Suddenly Wes remembered his mother urging him multiple times to study the material he should have memorized when he was sixteen. The royal laws and decrees. Wes pulled out his laptop and opened the document he'd downloaded over a week ago. He scanned through the ancient dialect, struggling to make sense of the meaning, but after thirty minutes of searching he found the section his mother must have wanted him to study.

By royal decree, the house of Riodan dictates that the first-born child will not automatically retain the right to be the crown prince or princess. The Montoya family is based on purity, intellect, goodwill, truth, and service to the people. All future kings and queens must display these attributes. In the case of special circumstances, His Royal Majesty and Her Royal Highness may invoke the edict of the heart of Riodan, which states that any heir not displaying the aforementioned attributes and a desire to serve the people for the greater good, may be removed from Royal standing, either temporarily or permanently. The right will then be passed on to the next worthy heir, not necessarily the next in birth order.

This edict is written to discourage unfavorable treatment of anyone in the royal family, regardless of their birth order.

Wes pushed his hand over his thick curls, reeling with the information he'd discovered. His mother and father must have been planning on invoking this edict for some time, which explained why his mother had encouraged him to study his royal heritage. He wondered why she hadn't simply told him about the edict. But another thought chased that one—she wanted him to understand the rules himself and see a different future than the one he thought was set in stone.

His heart tripped over the next beat. Elise said something about him being the favored prince. The articles he had scanned alluded to the same thing and even though he tried to deny it, he recognized the warnings his mother had given him. He recalled one of their conversations, *"Azacca was never a contender for the crown and with the choices that Titan is making, I doubt he will be much longer. Marius, however, could make a good king."*

So maybe he didn't need to worry. His brother Marius was only two years older than him, but he'd always carried an innate wisdom within. He would make a fine king when the time came. Wes stood and moved aside the heavy drapes to peek out the window. The lawn was covered with photographers and news crews. They were content to wait him out. Wes cursed the news people for ruining his perfect escape and that made him think of Elise. His stomach turned over with the acidic taste of betrayal. He turned away from the window and started packing his bags.

CHAPTER TWENTY-TWO

Thankfully, there were no reporters nearby when Elise returned home. She sprinted into the house, and the wind caught the door, slamming it shut behind her. The noise startled her and she slid against the door in a sobbing heap of tears. How could Amy do this to her? Elise pulled out her cell phone and sent several texts to Amy, accusing her of ruining her life, her chance at love with Wes, and for making him hate her forever. By the time she sent the tenth text, she felt her lungs loosening enough to draw a ragged breath. Two more breaths, and Elise decided she didn't want to hear what Amy had to say right now. She put her phone on silent and tucked it into her jacket pocket.

Gran walked into the kitchen humming, but stopped abruptly when she saw her granddaughter's tear-stained face. "Elise, what happened to you?"

Elise choked on another sob, shaking her head.

"I'm in the pit of despair!" she wailed.

"No, you're right here where you're supposed to be." Gran hugged her. "Let's figure this out together."

Elise cried as she told Gran everything that had happened. "And the worst part is that I fell in love with him, Gran. I'm an American. I knew it was probably just another *Roman Holiday* in the making and I let my heart get tangled up anyway."

Gran pulled her close and hugged her. "Your life is not a movie. I'm sorry this happened, but maybe it's better this way."

"This way?" Elise said. "Me without him. Why can't we be together?"

"A foreign prince." Gran tsked. "It would take a miracle."

"And why would that be such a bad thing, for something miraculous to happen in my life? Sometimes I think God enjoys punishing me," Elise cried.

"Now listen. God is not punishing you. He loves you," Grandma said. "God may be in charge, but we all still have the ability to choose and unfortunately, that means we often choose wrong and hurt the ones we love the most."

"But Wes wouldn't even listen to me. He blamed me for everything." Elise wiped her nose.

"Do you love him?"

"Gran," Elise protested, but it was feeble.

"True love is the greatest thing in the world," Gran said. "You need to call your prince and explain what you know and what you think happened."

"But he won't listen to me. He won't answer his phone."

"Then leave him a message, but do it now before the time pushes you farther apart from a chance at reconciliation."

Elise touched the top of her phone in her jacket pocket. Wes probably wouldn't answer because he was too angry, but would he be willing to consider a message once he'd cooled down? "I'll give him a chance to calm down and then I'll call."

Gran tsked. "It's better not to wait with matters of the heart."

Elise hugged her grandma. "If I could leave it all up to you, I'm sure my problems would be solved."

Gran chuckled. "You're a good girl. Something good will come of this even if it's not what you want right now."

Elise's heart tightened with those words. She didn't want Wes to be anything but the man that she'd fallen in love with—the man she thought loved her too. But Gran's wisdom pointed to the truth. If Wes didn't love her, then it was better for things to end now before her heart was so intertwined with his that it couldn't beat on its own. "I'm going up to my room for a few minutes."

Gran nodded and Elise climbed the stairs, curious as to how even lifting her foot to the next step seemed harder as if the events of that morning were pressing down on her, threatening to crush her into the ground like a giant in a wrestling match. She made it to her room and collapsed on her bed, staring up at the ceiling. The old plaster had bits of shimmer in it and as a child, Elise had often studied the grooves in the paint, finding shapes and animals. Now she wished that the bumps and ridges would rearrange themselves into a solution for her problem.

The phone was on the fourth ring and Elise took a breath to start her message when Wes answered. "Hello?" His voice was strained.

Elise gasped. "Wes, will you please listen to me for one minute? Sixty seconds is all I ask. I won't call again."

"Okay." His voice was sharp and impatient.

"You know who I am. I never hid that I'm human and make plenty of mistakes, but I did not betray you. I've been betrayed by someone I thought was a good friend. I'm sorry that I don't know how to fix this. I'm sorry that I told Amy about you and that I didn't anticipate what she was capable of. I do know that she had some pretty big bills she was trying to pay. I think maybe she grew desperate and decided to photograph you before someone else did. I am a victim here too. My friendship with Amy is over and look at what she's done to us."

"If you had warned me, we might have prevented this," Wes said.

"That's not true and you know it," Elise said. "I've told you the truth and now I'll tell you the rest. I didn't mean to, but I fell for you, and it wasn't because you're a prince or the hottest Montoya brother. It was because of your heart, your goodness, and the way you made me feel like a princess. I didn't want to admit it to myself, but things would have ultimately not worked out between us and this is as good a time as any to say our goodbyes. But first you need to know that I would never purposely hurt you, because I love you. Have a good life. I know you'll be a good leader."

Elise waited out two beats of silence and ended the call. She gripped her phone and wiped her eyes. Then she got up from her bed, straightened her clothes and headed back downstairs. Gran was in the kitchen, slicing up strawberries. Elise came and stood next to her at the sink. She popped a strawberry into her mouth and chewed slowly. "I need a miracle, but I need it now. I'm afraid Wes will leave and I'll never see him again."

"You rush a miracle man, you get rotten miracles,"

Grandma Suzy said. "Patience and love are the only miracles you need right now. If Wes is the man for you, he will listen, believe, and recognize that his judgements of you were wrong. If not, then he is not really a prince and it doesn't matter." Gran shrugged.

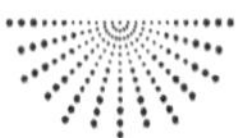

Thursday morning, Elise peeked out the window to check for any lingering news people, but the stories had all been told. Wes had left Echo Ridge in a private helicopter and Elise had stayed holed up until the reporters all left. The skies were blue with hints of sunlight filtering through white puffy clouds and Elise needed a breath of fresh air. She walked to the end of the lane toward the yellow mailbox.

Elise yanked the mailbox open and pulled out the stack of business envelopes. She flipped through them and found the one from the county assessor third from the top. Today didn't seem like the best day to open the letter, but it couldn't get much worse so she ripped open the envelope. Instead of a bill, there was a receipt of total payment and a credit balance with enough money to pay for at least ten years of taxes. She clutched the letter to her chest, not sure if she should believe it was true. Unfolding the letter again, she found a note that indicated there was no error in accounting, someone had paid the balance and future balance. Her throat tightened, and her eyes burned with tears of relief and wonder.

She'd been so preoccupied with the property tax statement, she'd almost missed the light lavender envelope addressed to Elise Gibson. She slipped her finger under the flap and carefully opened the envelope. She pulled out an ivory card with a beautiful watercolor of a purple hyacinth on the front. With a catch in her breath, she opened the card and read the bold script.

I'm sorry that I was a fool and didn't listen to you. But hear this now: I will always come for you.
    --Weston

Elise turned the card over and then read it again. What did it mean? He hadn't said he loved her, but that he would come for her. She walked back to the house, tucking the card away. "Gran, we finally have some good news."

An hour later, Elise sat on the couch looking at the soft green grass out the front window and trying to figure out what Wes had meant by sending that card. Gran was playing the piano, a jaunty tune that shared the joy they both felt after realizing that someone had rescued them from their financial problems. They both figured that person was a Riodanian prince and it made Elise's heart flood with hope.

Gran stopped playing the piano. "What's that noise?"

Elise stood and walked toward the humming sound that was now vibrating the windows. She opened the screen door and looked upwards. A black helicopter was descending to the pasture beside the front lawn. Two black SUVs pulled into the driveway.

"Is it your prince?" Gran asked.

"I hope so," Elise said. She stepped back inside and peered through the screen door, at the sleek helicopter that had just landed in front of her house. Her heartbeat felt like it was in her throat and she had to force herself to breathe as the blades slowed to a stop and the door of the helicopter popped open.

The tall, skinny security guard from the B&B exited first and then motioned to a dark-skinned man wearing a cream designer suit and dark sunglasses. He walked toward the house, holding something behind his back. He looked regal, refined, and definitely like royalty, but Elise would recognize him anywhere. When he saw her standing in the doorway, he flashed her a tentative smile. The dimple in his cheek made her stomach flip.

"May I speak with you for a moment?"

Elise pushed the screen door open and stepped back to let him inside. She could feel Gran giving Wes the stare-down behind her.

"Well, young man. I surely hope you have something good to say to my granddaughter, but I won't interfere." She turned to Elise. "I'll be out back for a few minutes."

"You don't have to leave Mrs. Gibson. I apologize for showing up like this."

Gran waved her hand. "Pish-posh. My flowers need tending to." She hurried out the back door before Elise could think of what to say. It didn't seem real that Wes was here, standing in front of her holding a bouquet of bright pink hyacinths, tied with a white ribbon. He extended the bouquet. Her nose twitched with the intoxicating smell. She took it with shaking hands and breathed in the aroma. "Thank you," she whispered and set them on the side-table, clasping her hands together.

"Elise, I'm so sorry." He took a step forward and put his hand over her fingers. "I lost my temper and I blamed you. It was wrong. I know you would never do something like that to me, but for some reason I forgot the truth."

Elise swallowed, allowing his words to settle on her heart and feeling the tingling warmth from his hand rising up her arms. "I'm really sorry how everything happened."

Wes shook his head. "You don't need to apologize. I acted like an idiot. Will you please forgive me?"

Elise nodded. "I forgive you, but how does that change things now? You left and I realize now that maybe I didn't understand even a tiny bit what it means to be a royal of Riodan."

"And I realized that it doesn't matter. None of it matters, because you're you and I need you and all of your wallpaper-removal skills and small-town upbringing."

She could see the need in his eyes, the spark of light that she loved shining as he smiled at her and moved his hands to her arms. Tears pooled and trickled over the rim of her lashes. "Oh, Wes, I don't know what to say."

"Well, I do." He put a finger on her chin and lifted her face to his. "I love you, Elise Gibson," he whispered before covering her mouth with a kiss.

That spark that Elise had felt during their first kiss was merely a warm glow compared to this kiss. Wes pulled her close and she put her arms around his neck, kissing him deeper, a thrill coursing through her middle and down to her toes. Wes caressed her back, gently moving her into a tighter embrace. Elise tipped her head back, breaking from his intoxicating kiss long enough to say, "I love you, too."

CHAPTER TWENTY-FOUR

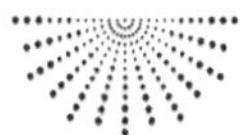

The news crews returned within the hour and Weston's security guards had to help them relocate off the property. Wes didn't seem bothered by the people and their cameras huddled in their vans waiting for the perfect shot. Elise couldn't get enough of his relaxed smile as they enjoyed a cup of tea while listening to the rain drizzle overhead.

"Whatever happened to Billy?" Gran asked with a twinkle in her eye.

Elise shook her head. "He was looking for something, but it wasn't me." She turned to Wes. "I already told Wes that I'm not interested in dating anyone else."

Wes grinned. "I'm glad you haven't changed your mind because I know that you've finished the remodeling of the theater room over at the B&B. If you can spare some time, I'd like to take you with me to Riodan to meet my family, my island, and my people."

Elise gulped a mouthful of the hot tea and closed her eyes as images of Riodan buzzed through her mind. It would be a dream come true, but then… she opened her eyes and turned to Gran.

"Oh no you don't." Gran shook her finger in the air. "You will not stay here to look after me when a prince wants to take you to his tropical island. I may be old but my ticker and my thinker still work fine."

"I'd like you to come along with her," Wes said.

Gran fanned her heart. "Well, bless my soul, he *is* a keeper." She turned to Wes. "I appreciate the offer, but I'd rather stay here for now. Maybe I can come for the wedding?"

Elise and Wes laughed. Elise reached out to squeeze his hand. "I would love to see Riodan."

"Will you come with me tomorrow?"

Elise's eyes widened, but she could almost hear Gran shooting down any reason she could come up with to postpone a trip. She grinned. "As you wish."

Wes leaned over and kissed her. "Thank you."

"For how long?"

"I won't be able to leave for some time. There's too much royal business to sort out with my family, but I'm hoping to keep you as long as possible." He winked.

"Keep me? On the island of Riodan? But I'm nobody,

and I'm an American. How will that ever work?" Elise sputtered.

"This is true love—you think this happens every day?"

Elise was nearly buzzing with the ideas that were taking root in her mind. Wes loved her and he wanted her to visit his royal home for as long as possible. She glanced at Gran who smiled serenely at her. Home had always been Echo Ridge, but Elise felt that she'd been preparing her whole life for something bigger than she could imagine. And now she was being offered a chance to love a man who was better than any fairy tale prince—mostly because he loved her in real life. She touched Wes's cheek. "No, it doesn't happen every day, but I'm glad it did today."

Wes grinned and pulled her in for another kiss.

Elise checked her list for the fourteenth time and crossed off two more items. It seemed impossible that she could be ready to leave on an extended vacation with only a day's notice, but her three suitcases were bulging. The passport she'd applied for last year would finally come in handy. A private jet was waiting to fly Wes and his new girlfriend to the island of Riodan.

Elise's stomach did cartwheels when she thought of herself as Wes's girlfriend.

When Elise was zipping up her suitcase, her phone pinged with a text. Her stomach clenched when she saw that it was from Amy.

I'm sorry. I didn't have any other options. If I hadn't taken the picture, someone else would have.

It wasn't much of an apology so Elise didn't respond. Amy would have to live with the choices she made. She and Wes had agreed to forgive her, but Elise felt disappointed that she had lost a friend. Pushing sad thoughts from her mind, Elise checked her watch and grinned because Wes would be arriving any minute. That thought was followed by the sound of him bounding up the stairs.

Elise turned as he entered her room and pulled her into an embrace. "You're early, and you look…" she cocked her head, "like someone who knows a pretty good secret."

Wes chuckled. "I want you to see something important." He took her hand and held up his smartphone. "Titan just gave a press conference. This is pretty big news."

Elise watched as the oldest Montoya prince looked out over a crowd of reporters and photographers. Titan was probably a couple inches taller than Wes, but he had the same dimple in his cheek that deepened when he smiled. He cleared his throat and began speaking, "Once the pressure of being king was gone, I realized that I could do something else with my life. I've always wanted to pursue my music. As King, there isn't time for frivolity and while I tried to embrace the stringent rules and guidelines while young, there came a time when I rebelled. I apologize for my behavior and what it has cost my family. I want the world to know that I accept responsibility for my actions and I'm making amends for everything I can. For the mistakes I can't fix, I am dedicated to living my life to make penance for those. I will not be returning to the palace.

"I accept and revere my parent's decisions to name Weston as crown prince. I love him and my family and I know that he will serve Riodan better than I ever could."

Elise jerked her head to look at Wes. "What? What about Marius?"

Wes shook his head. "Marius didn't want it. My parents and I have been talking. I don't think anything is official yet, and I'm pretty sure Titan wasn't supposed to share that information, but it is true. I'm willing to be the next king of Riodan. I hope that doesn't change things for us."

Elise opened her mouth and shut it. "I love you, but I could never get in the way of you being king. If you need me to stay here, I will."

Wes's eyebrows rose. "No, that's not what I meant. I

was trying to say that I hope you'll still give us a chance even though my life is changing."

Elise breathed a sigh of relief and nodded.

Wes pulled her close and kissed her forehead. "I need you more now than ever."

"As you wish." Elise tipped her head back and their lips met in a sweet kiss that held the promise of a future scattered with unknowns, but filled with love.

THE END

Amos's Honey Glazed Salmon

INGREDIENTS:

- 4 salmon filets
- Sea salt and freshly ground black pepper, to taste
- 4 tablespoons flour
- 4 tablespoons honey
- 2 tablespoons olive oil
- Zest of 1 lime

FOR THE LIME SAUCE

- 6 tablespoons unsalted butter
- 2 cloves garlic, pressed
- 1 tablespoon honey
- Juice of 1 lime
- Sea salt and freshly ground black pepper, to taste

DIRECTIONS:

1. Preheat oven to 400 degrees F.
2. To make the lime sauce, melt butter in a medium saucepan over medium heat. Cook,

whisking constantly, until the butter begins to turn a golden brown, about 3 minutes. Stir in garlic, honey and lime juice, salt and pepper, to taste; set aside.

3. Season salmon with salt and pepper, to taste. Dredge each salmon filet with 1 tablespoon flour and drizzle with 1 tablespoon honey.

4. Heat olive oil in a large oven-proof skillet over medium high heat. Working in batches, add salmon to the skillet and sear both sides until golden brown, about 1-2 minutes per side.

5. Place into oven and bake until completely cooked through, about 8-10 minutes.

6. Serve immediately with lime sauce and lime zest, if desired.

Bonus Sneak Peek

Want a sneak peek of the next Echo Ridge Romance? Read the first chapter of **Coming Home to Love** now! Available in print, ebook, and audio.

*L*aney Richins adjusted the cellophane around a dozen pink roses and inhaled the sweet scent. If only her life could be as uncomplicated and beautiful as roses. She pulled a crumpled petal away from one of the buds, her fingers lingering on the velvety texture. There was so much that Laney regretted, but like the rose, there was much more to her than the crumpled petals on the outside. With a shake of her head, Laney dismissed that train of thought and adjusted the silver ribbon.

She and her five-year-old son Oliver were happy in their little two-bedroom apartment. Happy to be far away from her ex-husband and just down the street from Grandpa and Grandma Richins. Laney didn't even mind the brunt of the summertime heat and humidity as August descended on Echo Ridge, New York. After eight years away, Laney had returned to her hometown—the same place she'd spurned and claimed she'd never come back to. She crouched down to snip a few wilted leaves from a fern and ended up sweeping up several of the tiny leaves from a low shelf. She had her head underneath the fronds of the fern when she heard the back door open. Maybe Paisley had forgotten something. Laney smiled, waiting for her sometimes-scatterbrained boss to call out.

"Laney?"

The person calling her name was definitely not Paisley Scott. It was a man, and she would know that voice anywhere, although it had matured to a more sultry tone. Even the note of surprise in the voice was recognizable. She turned slowly toward Billy Redford. His dark blond hair was cut short along the sides with a bit of a wave on top. He stood a head taller than her, at nearly six feet, and his skin was bronzed by the late summer sun. He was the same Billy from her high school days, but even better looking than her memories. His blue eyes widened, as if he hadn't believed it could really be her.

"Billy? What are you doing here?" She stood and brushed stray leaves from her knees, clenching her clippers tight enough in one hand that the handles bit into her skin.

"I came by to take some measurements for the new shelves Paisley needs."

Laney's heart pounded in her chest and her cheeks warmed at the sight of his broad shoulders and the scruff along his jawline. She couldn't figure out why he was measuring shelves for Paisley. The last she'd heard, Billy had graduated from college in construction management. "No, I meant, what are you doing here—as in Echo Ridge."

Billy arched an eyebrow. "I live here."

Laney's mouth dropped open. "Since when?"

"Almost a year ago." He tilted his head. "What are you doing here?"

"I moved back two weeks ago."

"No, I meant what are you doing here—as in Paisley's Petals."

Laney couldn't help but smile. Billy was teasing her just like old times—but no, that wasn't right. There was a look in his eyes that wasn't familiar. The way his jaw tightened as if he were biting back words made Laney take a step back. "I work here."

"Is this some kind of prank?" He turned and looked behind him. "I mean, you don't really want to live and work in Echo Ridge, do you?"

The words struck Laney like a bucket of water. They were words similar to those she'd thrown at Billy several times during their senior year. And then, that summer after graduation, she'd stomped on his dreams of staying in the small town to raise a family. She claimed that nothing could keep her in Echo Ridge and anyone who wanted to live and work there was small-minded.

She pulled her foot along the faded linoleum. "I deserve that I guess, but it's true nonetheless. I'm back in Echo Ridge to stay *and* I work here." Laney had never wanted to come back to Echo Ridge—the place where she was supposed to marry her high school sweetheart and raise her children. She'd turned her back on all of them, running after Dane and his sugar-sweet promises. She had Oliver and there was no regret there, but she wished she could undo other parts of her past.

Billy opened his mouth at the same time Paisley breezed into the shop. "Oh, hello, Billy. I'm glad you were able to make it in." She flipped her long brown braid over her shoulder and smiled. "I see you've met Laney. She and I were just talking earlier about how nice it will be to have some storage space. It's really nice of you to take this on. I know it's not what Redbuilt usually does."

Laney nodded, wondering if Paisley could pick up on the tension emanating between them. If she did, she chose to ignore it. She took Billy's arm and steered him toward the back wall while talking over her shoulder to include Laney. "Carlos has helped me in the past, but he's swamped and was kind enough to mention you."

"I don't mind," Billy answered. "We just poured the foundation for a new home by Ruby Mountain so my crew can handle things for a few days."

"Wait, who is Redbuilt?" Laney asked.

"It's my company," Billy answered. "Located *here* in Echo Ridge." His words had an edge to them and Laney caught the underlying jab again.

"That's marvelous. This town needs good construction companies. My parents mentioned how much it's growing, but I didn't believe them until I came home." She winked and was rewarded with a look of surprise from Billy. The bell over the front entrance rang, indicating a customer. "I'll help out front," Laney said. She walked away, knowing that just like old times, she'd been able to throw Billy for a loop. She had a genuine smile when she reached the customer.

Twenty minutes later, Laney finished an impromptu arrangement that Mrs. Tumnus needed for the library board meeting. The flowers were to celebrate Jennifer Staples finishing her degree in library science. Laney had seen her working in the young adult section of the library last time she went in. Once the silver-haired lady had exited the shop, Laney headed to the back to see what help she could offer Paisley. Her stomach clenched as she approached the area where Billy had been working, but her nerves unwound when she discovered he wasn't there.

"Looking for Billy?" Paisley poked her head around the corner. "He took some measurements and he won't be back until tomorrow night. Strange thing, that. Originally he'd planned to work all day tomorrow to get the project done, but suddenly he was too busy to be here during regular hours." Paisley arched an eyebrow in Laney's direction.

Laney shrugged. "That's probably for the best don't you think? Then we won't be tripping over each other."

Paisley snipped the end of a red rose and handed it to Laney. "They say every rose has a story and when it's given in love, the story is about the person who receives it."

"Hmm, I hadn't heard that before," Laney replied. "But you're the expert when it comes to flowers."

Paisley nodded and handed another rose to Laney. "True, you've only been here a couple weeks, but you have a gift with flower arranging, if you'll let yourself see it."

Laney looked down at the two roses, their buds barely beginning to open and spiral outward with velvet petals reaching toward the light. She lifted them to her nose and inhaled. "Thank you."

Paisley handed her three more roses. "If you'll add those to the Hyatt's funeral arrangement, I'll help you finish up."

Laney nodded and walked over to the refrigerated

unit that held several arrangements for the funeral. Winston Hyatt had been her seventh-grade science teacher and although he was in his late eighties, it was still hard to come to terms with the fact that people Laney had grown up around were dying. Those precious years of her childhood held magic, memories, and so much discovery. Every person in Echo Ridge had played a part in raising Laney Richins.

Even though she tried to convince herself it wasn't true, she couldn't help thinking that the best years of her life had been wasted and she wouldn't get a second chance to make the right choice. She didn't want to waste the chance this town was willing to give her. Everyone in Echo Ridge had opened their arms to the Laney they remembered, even if she was no longer that girl—everyone except Billy.

Continue reading Echo Ridge Romance #4, ***Coming Home to Love*** *available in ebook, print, and audio.* For more information visit

www.rachellechristensen.com

*This heart-warming, inspirational romance from award-winning and bestselling author Rachelle J. Christensen is part of the Echo Ridge Romance Collection.

Although you can read the books as standalones, you don't want to miss this exciting series:

Hope for Christmas
The Kiss Thief
The Princess Bride of Riodan
Coming Home to Love
Her Guy Next Door Fake Fiancé

ACKNOWLEDGMENTS

I'm so grateful for the many wonderful people who helped make this book possible. I especially appreciate you, the reader, for your encouragement and enthusiasm in Echo Ridge. A special thanks to beta readers, dozens who read my stories and cheered me on. A big thanks to my brilliant production team: Heather Justesen, Christina Dymock, Jenna Roundy, Gretchen, Jenn, and Leslie Ethington.

I'm grateful to my five beautiful children who keep me grounded and inspire me daily. A special thanks to my parents for their encouragement, support, and for being spectacular grandparents! Words can't express my thanks to my husband, Tyler, for his support of my writing. I'm so glad to have you in my corner.

And to you, the reader: Thank you for taking time to read my book. I know that there are so many to choose from, and I'm grateful that you were able to get to know the characters who feel like my friends now.

I'm especially grateful to God for blessing me in so many ways and encouraging me to see His hand in my life daily.

Rachelle J. Christensen

Photo by Erin Summerill

Rachelle writes mystery/suspense, clean romance, and women's fiction. She is the mother of a large family and she solves the case of the missing shoe on a daily basis. She enjoys raising chickens, laughing with her family, and traveling with her husband. She graduated cum laude from Utah State University with a degree in psychology and a minor in music.

Rachelle is the award-winning author of over twenty books, including *The Soldier's Bride (a Kindle Scout Selection)*, the Rone award winner for mystery, *River Whispers*, *Diamond Rings Are Deadly Things*, *Hawaiian Masquerade*, and *the Echo Ridge Romance series*. Her novella, "Silver Cascade Secrets," was included in the Rone Award–winning *Timeless Romance Anthology, Fall Collection*.

Join Rachelle's VIP mailing list to learn more about upcoming books and get your free book at www.rachellechristensen.com.

Thrills for the Heart

FOR A LIMITED TIME

**Sign up for Rachelle's
VIP Mailing List
to get your *FREE* book.**

★ ★ ★ ★ ★

Get started here:
www.rachellechristensen.com